HEADS, YOU LOSE!

GOOSEBUMPS HorrorLand™

ALL-NEW! ALL-TERRIFYING!

Also Available from Scholastic Audio Books

#1 REVENGE OF THE LIVING DUMMY

#2 CREEP FROM THE DEEP

#3 MONSTER BLOOD FOR BREAKFAST!

#4 THE SCREAM OF THE HAUNTED MASK

#5 DR. MANIAC VS. ROBBY SCHWARTZ

#6 WHO'S YOUR MUMMY?

#7 MY FRIENDS CALL ME MONSTER

#8 SAY CHEESE — AND DIE SCREAMING!

#9 WELCOME TO CAMP SLITHER

#10 HELP! WE HAVE STRANGE POWERS!

#11 ESCAPE FROM HORRORLAND

#12 THE STREETS OF PANIC PARK

GOOSEBUMPS HORRORLAND BOXED SET #1-4

WELCOME TO HORRORLAND: A SURVIVAL GUIDE

#13 WHEN THE GHOST DOG HOWLS

#14 LITTLE SHOP OF HAMSTERS

#15 HEADS, YOU LOSE!

Ride for your life in a pulse-pounding adventure with Goosebumps Horrorland™, the video game! Available now for Wii™, Nintendo DS™, and Playstation® 2!

GET GOOSEBUMPS PHOTOSHOCK FOR YOUR iPhone™ OR iPod touch®

GOOSEBUMPS®
NOW WITH BONUS FEATURES!

NIGHT OF THE LIVING DUMMY
DEEP TROUBLE
MONSTER BLOOD
THE HAUNTED MASK
ONE DAY AT HORRORLAND
THE CURSE OF THE MUMMY'S TOMB
BE CAREFUL WHAT YOU WISH FOR
SAY CHEESE AND DIE!
THE HORROR AT CAMP JELLYJAM
HOW I GOT MY SHRUNKEN HEAD
WEREWOLF OF FEVER SWAMP
A NIGHT IN TERROR TOWER
WELCOME TO DEAD HOUSE
WELCOME TO CAMP NIGHTMARE
GHOST BEACH
THE SCARECROW WALKS AT MIDNIGHT

GET MORE

ON DVD!

From Fox Home Entertainment

ATTACK OF THE JACK-O'-LANTERNS
THE HEADLESS GHOST
MONSTER BLOOD
A NIGHT IN TERROR TOWER
ONE DAY AT HORRORLAND
RETURN OF THE MUMMY
THE SCARECROW WALKS AT MIDNIGHT

HEADS, YOU LOSE!

R.L. STINE

SCHOLASTIC INC.
New York Toronto London Auckland
Sydney Mexico City New Delhi Hong Kong

ISBN 978-0-545-16196-1

Goosebumps book series created by Parachute Press, Inc.

12 11 10 9 8 7 6 5 4 3 2 1 10 11 12 13 14 15/0

Printed in the U.S.A. 40

First printing, May 2010

MEET JONATHAN CHILLER . . .

He owns Chiller House, the HorrorLand gift shop. Sometimes he doesn't let kids pay for their souvenirs. Chiller tells them, "You can pay me *next time*."

What does he mean by *next time*? What is Chiller's big plan?

Go ahead — the gates are opening. Enter HorrorLand. This time you might be permitted to leave . . . but for how long? Jonathan Chiller is waiting — to make sure you TAKE A LITTLE HORROR HOME WITH YOU!

PART ONE

I pulled my floppy blue cap down low on my forehead and gazed around Zombie Plaza. It was a hot, sunny day, and HorrorLand Theme Park was jammed with kids and families. “This is so awesome!” I said to my friend Ryan Chang. “Can you believe we finally made it here?” Ryan just nodded. He’s the quiet type. I could see my reflection in his round, silvery sunglasses. He never takes the sunglasses off.

Ryan wore a black T-shirt and black cargo shorts. He always wears black. Ryan is the shortest, shrimpiest kid in our class, but he’s totally cool.

“I think that’s the magic store over there,” I said, pointing across the plaza.

And a harsh, croaky voice rasped in my ear: *“Don’t point, Jessica. It’s not polite to point.”*

“Huh?” I spun around.

No one there.

I blinked. And then I figured it out.

Ryan laughed. "I got you."

"No way," I said. I gave his shoulder a hard shove. "I knew it was you."

Ryan can throw his voice. So can I. We're both really excellent ventriloquists. We're into magic tricks, too.

Ryan rubbed his shoulder. He straightened the shades over his eyes.

"Pick on someone your own size, Jessica," he muttered.

That's one of our little jokes since I'm nearly a foot taller than him. Ryan and I have a lot of little jokes. I guess it's because we've lived next door to each other since we were three.

We're twelve now, and it's like we're brother and sister. Sometimes we fight like a brother and sister. And sometimes we drive our other friends crazy by constantly playing tricks on each other. But most of the time we're cool together.

My name is Jessica Bowen, and you're probably wondering why Ryan and I are so into tricks and ventriloquism and stuff like that. Well, the answer is easy. My dad — sometimes known as The Amazing Billy Bowen — is a birthday party ventriloquist and magician.

He does three or four birthday parties a week. He's very popular. Sometimes he's even on TV.

Dad taught us how to throw our voices when we were five. Ryan and I used to put on magic shows when we were in second grade!

And that's why the magic shop was our first stop at HorrorLand.

We took off across the plaza and almost ran into a green-and-purple food cart. The sign on the side read: CHIHUAHUA TENDERS. MADE WITH REAL CHIHUAHUA BITS!

"That's sick," I said. We have two Chihuahuas at home named Abra and Cadabra. They are part of Dad's magic act. He pulls them out of his coat sleeves. The dogs love it.

The magic shop stood next to a big theater. In dark ghostly letters the marquee read: THE HAUNTED THEATER. MONDO THE MAGICAL — NOW APPEARING (AND DISAPPEARING)!

"Awesome. Let's see when the next show goes on," I said.

But Ryan was already hurrying into the shop.

I pulled open the door, and two kids rushed out. One of them was holding a huge deck of cards. The other had one of those fake little guillotines in his hand. The kind where you put your finger in. Then you push down on the blade, and it looks like it slices off your finger.

It's a pretty good trick. I think Ryan and I learned it when we were four.

The shop looked small on the outside, but it stretched really far back. I could see two long aisles with shelves and shelves of magic tricks. A shiny suit of armor stood at the end of one aisle. It had a magic wand gripped in its metal glove. A stuffed rabbit poked out from the open visor.

"Jessica, check out these chains and padlocks," Ryan said. He tugged at a heavy silver lock, and it popped right open. "Perfect for quick escapes."

He turned to me. "Does your dad ever do an escape from a locked trunk?"

"No way," I said. "That's too scary for kids."

Dad has to be careful. If he makes the kids cry, he won't be invited to perform at many birthday parties!

I picked up a pair of Chinese puzzle rings. I slapped them together, then pulled them apart. Easy.

I turned and saw Ryan pick up a metal cuff. It looked like it had sharp teeth. "This is a mean-looking handcuff," he said.

I opened a box of playing cards. I pulled out the deck and examined it. Every card in the deck was the ace of spades.

I started to put the cards back when I heard a deafening *SNAP*.

Then I heard a scream.

I turned — and saw the metal cuff clamped around Ryan's wrist.

"Jessica, HELP ME!" he shrieked. "It HURTS! It HURTS! Ohhh, help! MY HAND IS BROKEN!"

2

Of course, I didn't fall for it.

Ryan is a good actor. But he's tried this kind of gag too many times to fool me. I didn't even flinch. Really.

"Where's the blood?" I asked.

Ryan shrugged. "Hey, I almost got you."

"No, you didn't," I said. I grabbed his arm and pried the metal cuff off. I snapped it a few times between my hands. "Sweet."

Ryan backed away from me. I didn't like the grin on his face. "What?" I said. "Come on. What's so funny?"

He didn't answer. Instead, he reached into his back pocket and pulled out a pink cell phone.

My phone!

"You thief!" I cried. "You pickpocket! How did you get that?"

His grin grew wider. "It's easy if you're *good*."

I could see my reflection in his silver sunglasses. I looked angry. "Give it back," I said.

He started to hand the phone to me. Then, as I grabbed for it, he swung it out of my reach.

"Hey! Not funny!" I said. I gave him a shove. I didn't mean to push him that hard. Sometimes I forget how light he is.

He went flying backward — and tumbled right into a big man just entering the shop. The man wore a black tuxedo, bow tie, and top hat. Mondo the Magical!

Mondo had a round red face under slicked-down black hair. He had a bushy black mustache that seemed to sprout from his huge nose. His nose looked just like a lightbulb!

He stared at us. His bushy eyebrows wriggled up and down like caterpillars. His tuxedo shirt bulged over his big belly.

"Do you want to buy that handcuff trick?" he asked me. He had a deep, growly voice.

I gazed down at it. I didn't realize I was still holding it. "Uh . . . no," I said. I dropped it onto the shelf. "Just looking at it."

"It's a good trick," Mondo said. "It'll make your parents scream."

"I don't think so," I said.

He sighed and pulled off the top hat. His black hair glistened with sweat. "Did you kiddos catch my show?" he asked.

"Not yet," Ryan said. "But we want to. We're totally into magic."

Mondo nodded. "The last one was the worst show I ever did," he muttered. He waggled his hands. "I'm totally butterfingers today. Even my best trick went wrong."

"What's your best trick?" I asked.

"The one where I pull a hat out of a rabbit," he said.

He set the hat down on a counter. Then he pulled a live rabbit out from under his tuxedo jacket. "Would you believe the rabbit started to gag? I couldn't get the hat out!"

Shaking his head, he carried the rabbit to a cage against the wall.

"My dad says sometimes the spirits of magic are just against you," I said.

Mondo spun around. "Who is your dad?"

"He's a magician, too," I said. "He does birthday parties back home in Tampa."

Mondo's eyes flashed, and his fat eyebrows rolled up and down. "Maybe you'd like to buy your dad a new magic trick? I've got some tricks you kiddos have probably never seen before. I collect them from all over the world — and some from other planets!"

I glanced around at the shelves of tricks. "They look pretty expensive," I said.

Ryan picked up a thick rope. One end was tied

in a loop. Ryan is totally into rope tricks. He ties knots in a rope. Then he shakes the rope and the knots magically disappear.

"That's a very good rope trick you've got there," Mondo said. "One of my best. This trick was handed down from the ancient first Raja of the Kingdom of Gold."

He took the rope from Ryan's hand. "Bet your dad doesn't know this one," he said to me.

"How does it work?" Ryan asked.

"Watch." Mondo lowered the loop around his big waist. Then he tightened it like a belt.

"Here. Take this," he told Ryan. He handed Ryan the other end. "See? I've got the loop around me. Now, pull the rope as hard as you can. Give it a good tug."

"And what will happen?" Ryan asked. "Do you make the loop disappear?"

"That's too easy," Mondo replied. "I make the *whole rope* disappear!"

"Cool," I said. I reached out and gave the rope a squeeze. It was a real rope. How was Mondo going to make it disappear right from Ryan's hands?

Ryan gripped the rope in both hands. He gave it a hard tug.

"Go ahead. Pull. Pull!" Mondo ordered. "Pull it with all your strength."

Ryan gave another hard tug. He backed down the long aisle, pulling the rope.

Mondo shut his eyes. He grunted and groaned. "Pull. Pull." He strained against the rope belt.

Ryan tugged again.

The rope didn't vanish.

Mondo opened his eyes. His face was red. He had droplets of sweat on his forehead. "Not my day," he said with a sigh. "Let's try another trick." He lifted the loop over his head and tossed the rope onto the floor.

He mopped his forehead with the back of his hand. "What's your name, kiddo?" he asked me.

"Jessica," I said. "Jessica Bowen."

"Well, you're right, Jessica," he said. "Some days the spirits of magic are against you."

He turned and started down the aisle. His tuxedo pockets bulged. I could see he had a lot of stuff hidden in them. "I know I have some tricks you will love," he said.

I noticed a long box lying flat on the floor. The lid was decorated with hand-painted red and yellow flowers.

"What's this wooden box?" I asked. "It looks like a coffin."

"It's called the Forever Box," Mondo said. He lifted the lid. The inside of the box was lined in red velvet. "If you lie in this box and I close the lid, you disappear *forever*."

"How does it work?" I asked.

"Show us," Ryan said. He jumped into the box.

He settled onto his back. He's so small, he fit with room to spare.

"You sure?" Mondo asked.

"Sure," Ryan said.

Mondo started to lower the lid. He gazed at me. "Say good-bye to your friend — forever."

Ryan and I both laughed.

We didn't know that was the beginning of all the horror.

Mondo leaned down and spoke to Ryan. "Cross your arms tightly over your chest," he said. "You are about to take a long journey. Do you have any last words?"

"Live long and prosper!" Ryan cried. What a goof.

"Excellent last words," Mondo said.

He kept his eyes on me as he slowly lowered the lid. It shut with a soft *whump*. Mondo pushed back the tails of his tuxedo jacket. Then he leaned over the box and muttered some magical words. "Vanno . . . vanno . . . *vanish*!"

He's so cornball, I thought. *My dad would think this was a riot.*

"Go ahead, Jessica," Mondo said, stepping back. "Pull open the lid of the Forever Box."

I gripped the edge with both hands and raised the lid.

Sure enough, Ryan was gone.

I bent down and tapped the sides of the box. Solid wood.

"Sweet," I said. I stood back up and turned to Mondo. He had a toothy grin under his mustache. "The box has a fake bottom, right?" I asked.

"No. Not right," Mondo said. "The back panel is fake. It slides open. Go ahead. Slide it. Your friend is behind it."

I leaned over the front of the box. I saw a little handle down low on the back panel. I grabbed it and slid the panel open.

No Ryan.

Mondo and I both stared at the empty hidden compartment.

I laughed. "Awesome!" I said. "Where is he hiding? Is there another hidden compartment?"

But Mondo's smile had faded. His eyebrows crinkled up until they mashed into one furrowed eyebrow. "Whoa," he muttered. He stared down at the empty box. "Whoa."

"Where is he?" I repeated.

Mondo gently moved me aside. Then he pushed back his jacket again and carefully squeezed into the box. He got down on his hands and knees and began tapping all the sides with the back of one hand.

"Hey, kiddo!" he shouted. "Kiddo — where are you? Are you playing a trick on the magician?"

I crossed my arms in front of me and watched. I really didn't know what to think. Mondo *had* to be putting on an act. This was just a trick. He was showing off his acting skills. Trying to scare me.

"Kiddo — you can come out now!" Mondo boomed. He tapped the sides some more. "This isn't funny."

Finally, he grabbed the front of the box and hoisted himself to his feet. His face was pale, dripping with sweat. He shook his head.

"Where *is* he?" he murmured, talking to himself.

Then he turned to me. "This is no joke," he said. "This has never happened to me. Your friend is *gone*!"

I started to laugh. But the expression on his face made me stop. Why was he trembling like that?

Was he *serious*?

He wiped sweat from his mustache. Then he slowly climbed out of the box. "I don't understand . . . I don't understand," he muttered. "It's a simple trick."

I knelt next to the box and checked for a fake bottom. No. I couldn't find one.

"Ryan?" I called. "Ryan? Are you in there?"

No answer.

I felt a chill at the back of my neck. My mouth suddenly felt dry. I stood up and turned to Mondo.

He had pulled off his tuxedo jacket. His white shirt had big sweat stains under the armpits. "It's a bad-luck day," Mondo said softly. "I should never have tried that trick."

I grabbed his sleeve. "But it's just a trick,

right? Let's get serious here. Ryan didn't really disappear into thin air."

Another chill at the back of my neck.

"Are your parents in the park?" Mondo asked. "Do you have a cell phone? I think you'd better call them."

"Huh?" My mouth dropped open.

Mondo's eyes locked on mine. "We have a real problem here," he said. "I wish I was joking, Jessica. But I'm not."

I swallowed. My mouth felt like cotton. My mind whirred with all kinds of crazy thoughts.

I'm not the kind of girl who gets scared. I don't scream at scary movies. And I'm not afraid to touch bugs or snakes.

My dad says I'm either brave or nuts.

He means it as a compliment.

But staring at Mondo, with his pale face and trembling hands, I felt afraid.

"Call your parents," he said.

I shook my head. "No. I know how to find Ryan," I told him.

He squinted at me. "You do?"

"Yes," I said. "Send me there, too. Do the trick with me."

I didn't wait for him to argue. I stepped into the box and lowered myself inside.

"I don't like this," Mondo said. "I don't like this at all."

"Close the lid," I said. "I'll find Ryan. No problem."

Mondo sighed. "It's not my day," he murmured again.

I settled onto my back and crossed my arms over my chest. The box smelled like pine. The velvet tickled my legs.

"Come on! Do it!" I shouted.

The lid slowly closed over me. I blinked in the total darkness. The air instantly became heavy and hot.

Above me, I could hear Mondo saying the magic words. Muffled by the wooden lid, he sounded miles away.

I waited with my eyes wide open, staring into the blackness. I realized I was holding my breath. I exhaled in a long whoosh.

And suddenly, I felt myself start to slide.

The bottom of the box dropped away.

I let out a sharp cry as I slid down . . . down. On my back, my hands flailing in the air.

I was on a slippery, steep slide, picking up speed. Sailing down . . . faster . . . faster . . . into a deep darkness.

5

I screamed all the way down. My voice echoed as if I were sliding down a deep well.

It seemed as if I slid for hours. But it was probably less than a minute.

Where was it taking me?

When would it end?

My scream ended in a hiccup as I came to a stop.

The slide let me off gently. I landed on my feet. Total blackness all around.

Where am I? I wondered.

My heart was pounding like a drum. I took a deep breath. Then I cupped my hands around my mouth and shouted, "Ryan? Hey — Ryan?"

No answer.

My eyes slowly adjusted to the darkness. I saw a dim light. I started to walk toward it. My legs felt shaky, and my heart was still thudding away.

A narrow metal ladder stood in front of me. I nearly walked right into it.

I gripped the sides of the ladder and gazed up. I saw a square opening above me. And the glare of white light.

I squeezed both hands tightly on the ladder and began to climb. My shoes slapped the metal rungs and made them ring. I pulled myself to the top and stepped out of the darkness into the square of bright light.

"Ryan?"

He stood in front of me. I couldn't see his eyes behind the silvery shades, but he looked dazed.

"Ryan? You're okay?"

He nodded. "I guess."

"Where are we?" I asked, squinting in the bright light.

He didn't have to answer. I could see we were at the back of a store.

I took a few steps down the aisle. The shelves were crammed with souvenirs and joke items — stuffed monkeys and rubber chickens, skulls with glowing red eyes . . .

"A gift shop," Ryan said, shaking his head. "Do you believe it? That big phony sent us to a gift shop."

I chuckled. "Mondo sure had me fooled. I thought something terrible happened to you. He may be a lousy magician, but he's a terrific actor. I really thought he was scared!"

"He just wanted to sell us stuff," Ryan grumbled.

I picked up a cute brown-and-white stuffed puppy. "PUT ME DOWN!" it screamed.

Startled, I dropped it back on the shelf.

Ryan laughed. "Cool. Pick it up again."

I picked up the little puppy. "I'LL BITE YOUR FACE!" it shrieked.

We both laughed.

I picked up a greenish skull. It was made of wax or something. "Hey, I think it's a candle," I said. "A skull candle."

"Do you like that?" a voice asked.

I turned to see an old man in an old-fashioned suit and vest. He had thin gray hair swept back off his forehead. Square eyeglasses perched on the end of his long nose.

He looked a lot like the picture of Benjamin Franklin in my history textbook.

"Yes, it's nice," I said. I started to put it down, but it stuck to my hand.

"It's a very special skull," the old man said in a croaky voice. "It's actually a man trap. It was used by a long-lost tribe of island warriors. Sadly, they took the secret of making the wax with them."

I struggled with the candle. The wax was melting and sticking to my hand. It was growing hot. I tried to push it off my hand with my other hand. But the wax spread and tightened over my skin.

The old man chuckled. "Don't fight it. The more you struggle, the more you heat it up."

"Well, what do I do?" I cried. "Get it off me!"

He adjusted the square spectacles on his nose. His blue eyes flashed. "You have to know the secret cure," he said. "Just blow on it."

I didn't hesitate. The hot wax was covering my hands like tight gloves. I blew on my hands as hard as I could.

And the green wax let go of me and rolled up into a tight ball the size of a golf ball.

"That is so awesome!" Ryan exclaimed. He took the little ball from me. "We have GOT to buy one of these and spring it on Boomer."

Boomer is a big bully of a kid who is always in our faces. Boomer likes to pound us and take our lunch money and give Ryan and me a hard time.

I rolled my eyes. "For sure, Ryan. We'll give him one of these. And then what will Boomer do to us? Turn *us* into wax skulls?"

Messing with Boomer was always a mistake. We both had the bruises to prove it.

"Allow me to introduce myself," the old man croaked. He straightened his floppy black bow tie. "My name is Jonathan Chiller, and this is my shop, Chiller House."

"Nice place," I said. My hands still throbbed a little from the hot wax.

"May I show you some interesting souvenirs I think you will like?" Chiller asked.

He gazed over the shelves and picked up a very real-looking bat. Its eyes glowed red, and its mouth was open as if ready to bite someone. He moved his hand up and down rapidly, and the bat's wings flapped.

"It's actually a kite," he said. "But you can't see the string. When the wind blows through it, it shrieks. Fly this into a crowd and you can *terrify* people. It's so real."

"Sweet," Ryan said. He rubbed the bat's stomach. "Feels like real fur."

I searched a low shelf and found something I liked. "Ryan, check it out," I said. I rolled it in my hand.

A two-headed gold coin. About the size of a quarter.

It had a man's face on both sides. I didn't know who it was.

"Ryan, this coin is perfect for magic tricks," I said.

He grinned. "And awesome for winning bets!" he said. "*Heads, I win — tails, you lose!* It always comes up heads!"

Jonathan Chiller chuckled. "Yes. You'll win every bet with that coin," he said.

"I definitely need to buy this," I told the old man. "Do you have another one for my dad?"

He frowned. "I'm so sorry. There is only one like it in the whole world."

"Well, I'll take it," I said. "Ryan and I will have a lot of fun with this." I handed it to Chiller.

"Let me wrap that for you," Chiller said. He carried it to the front counter. He wrapped the coin in black paper. Then he tied a red ribbon around it.

I watched him attach a little figure to the ribbon. It was a tiny green-and-purple Horror. It looked just like all the park guides and workers at HorrorLand.

Chiller smiled. "Take a little Horror home with you," he said to me. He handed me the package.

I reached into my shorts pocket for my money. "How much do I owe you?" I asked.

He waved me away. "No, no," he said. "No charge now. You can pay me back next time you see me."

I stared at him. *Next time?*

What did he mean by that?

PART TWO

A week later, I was back home. When I came down to breakfast, Dad was flipping the two-headed coin. Still yawning, I dropped down beside him at the breakfast counter.

"Heads or tails?" Dad said.

"Good morning to you, too," I replied.

He grinned. "Good morning, Jessica. Heads or tails?"

I rolled my eyes. "Dad, you and I both know —"

He spun the coin in front of my face. "Winner gets five dollars. Heads or tails?" he said.

"Okay," I said. "Heads."

He rolled the coin in his hand. He made a fist. Then he flipped it into the air. It bounced onto the counter. Bounced again. And landed on its side!

I let out a shriek. "How did you do that?"

He laughed. "Do what? The coin did it!"

"Can you teach me that trick?" I asked.

He took a long sip of coffee. Then he made a face. He pretended to choke. Then he reached between his lips and pulled out the coin.

I shook my head. "That's an old one," I said.

He shrugged. "An oldie but a goodie."

Dad is thin and wiry. Everything about him is slender. His parents used to call him Broom because he was as skinny as a broom.

He has wavy brown hair with just a little gray at the sides. Warm brown eyes and a warm smile. The first thing people notice about Dad is his hands. That's because they are so big, with very long fingers.

Dad says with those hands, he could have been a great piano player. Except he has no musical talent at all. He can't even hum!

But his long, slender hands are perfect for performing magic. He can hide anything in them. And he can switch coins or cards faster than a human can see.

Mom is tall and big, like me. Big-boned. That's what she calls it. And she and I have the same straight brown hair and blue eyes.

I spooned down some Cheerios. Dad slid the two-headed coin between his fingers. "I'll show you another trick," he said.

He placed the coin flat in the palm of his hand. "Now, watch, Jessica. I'm going to make the coin flip over without moving a muscle."

I glanced up from my cereal bowl — and my

eye caught the flower clock on the kitchen wall. "Oh, no!" I cried. "Dad — I'm going to be late!"

I grabbed the coin and jumped to my feet. Dad was always doing this to me. Showing off trick after trick and making me late for school.

"Later!" I called. I slid the coin into my shorts pocket, grabbed my backpack off the front stairs, and ran out of the door.

The sun was rising over the houses. The grass sparkled. A typical Tampa morning, already hot and humid.

My school is only two blocks away from my house, but I knew I'd be sweaty by the time I got there. I didn't care. Mrs. Leewood had already warned me a few times about coming in late.

I squeezed between the twin palm trees on the corner. I do it every morning. Don't ask me why. It's just a superstition I have.

Then I ran full speed down the next block, a block of little redwood houses. The playground came into view. Nearly empty. Almost everyone was inside the school.

I saw a few stragglers jogging toward the doors. And then I stopped — and gasped. "Oh, no . . ."

Boomer had Ryan pushed up against a tree. He held Ryan by the shirt with one big hand and waved his other fist in front of Ryan's face.

Was I too late to save him?

I went running toward them, shouting. The backpack bounced hard against my back.

Boomer didn't even turn around.

He pulled his fist back — and drove it hard into Ryan's stomach.

Ryan made a *gaaaack* sound. He dropped to his knees. His sunglasses fell to the grass. He bent over, hugging himself.

"Boomer — you jerk!" I shouted angrily.

He turned. He had a toothy grin on his fat face. He likes punching kids. Boomer spends a lot of time punching kids or threatening to punch them.

Boomer is big and wide. He has tiny brown eyes close together above his piggy snout of a nose, and his two front teeth poke out of his mouth. He has very short rust-colored hair and dark freckles all over his face.

He has a hoarse, squeaky voice. Like chalk on

a chalkboard. He doesn't sound tough, but trust me, he's tough.

Know his favorite superhero? You guessed it — The Incredible Hulk.

Boomer lives in some kind of fantasy world. He really thinks he *is* the Hulk! That makes him dangerous to us normal non-mutants.

"Why did you hit Ryan?" I cried, out of breath from running.

"He made a joke," Boomer said. "I don't like jokes."

"Your parents made a joke!" Ryan said. "It's YOU!"

Why does Ryan have to make Boomer mad? Why can't he just hand over his lunch money like everyone else and keep his mouth shut?

All Boomer wants is money. That, and to see kids shake when he struts by doing his Hulk imitation. Everyone is afraid of him, too afraid to report him to Mrs. Leewood, our teacher, or Mr. Greene, the principal.

"Funny," Boomer said. He pulled Ryan to his feet. "I told you, I don't like funny."

He raised his fist and got ready to deliver another punch.

I dove forward and grabbed his hand. "Wait, Boomer."

He spun around. His face turned bright red. "What's *your* problem, Jessica?" he squeaked.

"You don't want to get in the way of my fist — *do* you?"

"I have an idea," I said. My heart started to pound.

"I have an idea, too," Boomer said. He stuck out a hand. "Pay up."

"Give me a second," I said. "You'll like this. It's cool. We'll flip a coin."

Boomer wiped spit off his chin. "Maybe I'll flip *you*," he growled.

"We'll flip a coin," I repeated. "One toss. If you win, Ryan and I will give you lunch money every day for a week. And . . . if I win, you'll let Ryan and me go."

He stared at me with his tiny brown eyes. I could see his big freckled forehead crinkling. I knew he was thinking hard.

"Come on. Let's try it," I said. I slid the gold coin from my shorts pocket. "One toss. If you win, it's money for a whole week. What can you lose?"

"You can lose some teeth," Boomer muttered.

He's like a bad cartoon. A SCARY bad cartoon.

I held the coin up. It gleamed in the sunlight. "Want to give it a try?" I asked.

I hoped he didn't see my hand trembling. Ryan had his eyes on the coin. He knew what was happening. I could see him struggling not to smile.

Boomer nodded. "Go ahead, Jessica. Toss it."

"Here goes," I said, raising the coin higher. "Heads, I win."

I flipped the coin high in the air. It came down quickly and bounced twice on the playground grass.

The three of us leaned over it. "Heads," I said. "You lose, Boomer."

I started to shove the coin back into my pocket. Boomer grabbed my wrist. "Again," he said. "That was just practice. Now let's do it for real."

I hesitated. "Come on, Boomer. You agreed —"

He clapped his sweaty hand over my mouth. "Again," he said.

I backed away from him. "Okay, okay. Here goes." I flipped the coin even higher this time. "Heads, I win," I said.

"Tails, you lose," Ryan muttered.

It landed in front of Boomer's huge sneakers. He squinted down at it. "Heads."

Ryan and I cheered.

Boomer muttered some nasty words. His face turned bright red again. He spit on the grass. Then he spun around and stomped away toward school.

Ryan and I waited till he was in the building. We didn't dare laugh or say anything. What if Boomer decided to come back for a *third* coin toss?

Finally, we couldn't hold it inside any longer. We let out a victory cheer.

I heard the bell ring inside the school. "We're late," I said. "Better hurry."

I bent down to pick up the coin. I didn't see it. I began to crawl, searching the grass with both hands.

No coin.

"Where is it?" I cried, starting to panic. "Did Boomer take it?"

"I don't think so," Ryan said. He was squatting with his head down, searching, too.

"Hey — that shiny thing —"

We spotted the coin at the same time in a thick clump of grass.

We both dove and made a grab for it.

I wrapped my fingers around it. Ryan's hand wrapped around mine.

And suddenly, I felt weird. Dizzy. The grass tilted up toward me. The sky tilted away.

"Hey!" I uttered a sharp cry. Ryan's hand slipped away.

The grass spun under me. So dizzy . . . Did my feet leave the ground? Was the whole playground flying above me?

I felt as if I were being flipped over. Flipped over and over — tossed like a coin.

I tried to cry out again, but the sound caught in my throat.

The green grass and blue sky whirled and spun in front of my eyes.

And I was whirling and spinning, too. Flipping head over heels.

"*Ow.*" I landed sitting up with a hard thud.

I blinked several times, trying to clear my head. Trying to blink away my dizziness.

It took a few moments to get my eyes to focus. Sitting in the grass, I gazed all around.

Where was my school? Where was the playground?

Dazed, I murmured to myself: "Everything has changed."

I climbed shakily to my knees. I seemed to be in a wide, empty field. Tall grass swayed all around me. It looked like ocean waves, a sea of grass.

A flock of large birds floated silently overhead. They cast a fluttering shadow over me.

"Where are we?"

I heard a voice behind me. Startled, I whipped around — and saw Ryan sitting cross-legged on the grass.

"Ryan? You're here!" I cried.

He pulled off the sunglasses and squinted at me. "Yes, I'm here," he said. "But where is *here*? Where is the school?"

I stood up. I walked over and pulled him to his feet. We were both wobbly. I still felt dizzy.

"Did you feel like you were spinning?" I asked him. "Flipping over and over?"

He nodded. "Jessica, let's find the street. If we can see the street, we'll know where we are."

"Sounds like a plan," I said.

I shielded my eyes with my hand. I gazed all around. "I don't see any streets," I said.

Ryan made a gulping sound. "Weird," he murmured.

We started to walk. The tall, swaying grass brushed our legs. Insects buzzed and chirped all around us. Another silent flock of birds floated overhead.

"Where is our school?" I said. My voice came out shrill and tight.

"I don't like this," Ryan said in a whisper.

A gust of wind made the grass slap my legs. It seemed like the whole world was swaying, bending one way, then the other. An endless green world.

"Maybe, somehow, we got sent back to prehistoric times," Ryan said. "And we're the only two living humans."

I gave him a shove. "That's great, Ryan. I knew I could count on you to look on the bright side."

He started to reply — then stopped with his mouth open. He pointed straight ahead.

I turned and saw a gray line in the distance, cutting through the grass.

"Is that a street?"

No. As we hurried closer, it came into clear view. A wall. Taller than us. Made of flat gray stone. It stretched in a straight line through the grass as far as I could see.

Ryan pulled a green bug off his cheek and tossed it away. The bug had a hard, round body and at least sixty spindly little legs!

"Why would someone build a wall in the middle of this field?" Ryan asked.

I felt a sting on my forehead. I slapped a green bug off. It left a sticky juice on my skin.

I brushed two more of the fat bugs off the legs of my jeans. "The grass is *infested* with these creepy bugs," I groaned.

I shivered. My back tingled. Bugs crawling up my back?

Ryan turned and began jogging along the side of the wall. I followed after him. "Wait!" I called. "Ryan — stop!"

He stopped and turned around. "We have to go one way or the other," he said.

I shook my head. A green bug fell out of my hair. "I've had enough," I said. "Enough mystery. I'm getting us out of here."

Ryan mopped sweat off his forehead. He leaned against the stone wall. "How?" he demanded.

I swung my backpack in front of me. Two fat green bugs were climbing on the straps. I slapped them away.

I pulled my phone out. "Dad is home today," I said. "I'm calling him to come get us."

I pushed the speed-dial number for my home and waited for Dad to answer.

Silence.

It didn't ring at the other end.

I pushed STOP. Then tried again.

Silence.

I raised the phone and studied it. The screen was dark. I pushed the power button. Nothing happened.

"Maybe the battery is dead," Ryan said.

"No way!" I replied. "I charged it this morning."

I pushed a few more buttons. Still nothing happened. With a sigh, I shoved the phone back into the backpack.

The strong sun beamed down on us, but I was shivering. I'm not easily frightened. But this was just too freaky.

My leg itched. I scratched it and felt a squish under my shorts. Another green bug, I guessed.

"Jessica —" Ryan started. "Maybe . . ."

A horse whinnied.

We stared at each other.

"Did you hear that?" I said.

The horse whinnied again.

Ryan tapped the wall. "It's on the other side," he said. "Maybe there are people there, too."

The wall was about two or three feet taller than me. "Give me a boost," I said.

Ryan frowned. "You're going over the wall? How will I get over?"

"Didn't you bring a ladder?" I joked. "You're so short, you need a ladder to brush your hair!"

"Ha-ha." Ryan made a disgusted face. "That's one of your dad's worst jokes."

The horse whinnied again.

"Boost me up to the top, and I'll pull you up," I said. "Come on — hurry. You want to get home, don't you?"

"If we still *have* homes," Ryan muttered.

He bent down and cupped his hands like a stirrup. I lowered my sneaker into his hands, and he lifted me up high enough to grab the top of the wall.

I hoisted myself up. The top of the wall was about two feet wide. I balanced on my knees. Then I bent and helped Ryan scramble up beside me.

On our knees on the wall, we both turned — and uttered cries of shock.

"Ryan, where *are* we?"

"A castle!" I cried. I pointed into the distance.

A steamy mist clung to the ground. The building shimmered over the mist, pink and purple, like a fairytale castle.

A wide yellow path led to the castle doors. A huge black-and-red banner fluttered on a tall flagpole high over the entrance.

The building seemed to stretch for a mile, with pointed spires and tall towers on each end.

"It looks like the castle at Disney World," Ryan murmured. "Unreal!"

"Unreal is the word," I said. "How can this be happening? What happened to our school? Our neighborhood? Our houses?"

We gazed at the shimmering castle. Then we turned and lowered ourselves to the ground.

In front of us, a narrow wooden bridge arched over a thin sliver of water. On the other side of the bridge, I saw a row of small shacks. The shacks appeared to be slapped together with boards and gray mud. They had thatched roofs. No doors or windows — just square openings cut into the walls.

Ryan and I strode across the bridge. The water beneath us was dark and still. The horse whinnied once more.

"It's over by those shacks," I said, pointing. "Let's find someone to help us."

There was no tall grass on this side of the wall. Here, the ground was yellow dirt. Our shoes kicked up clouds of dust as we trotted toward the row of shacks.

I saw a fire, orange flames dancing in the soft breeze. A man stood working beside the fire.

He was a big, powerful-looking man wearing a ragged outfit — a vest over his bare chest and baggy trousers that looked like they were made from an animal hide.

He had long, scraggly hair that fell over his dark eyes, and a thick brown beard. His face was red and sweaty.

He didn't see us. He was concentrating on the tool in his hands. It had two handles, and he was squeezing it over the fire.

I recognized it from a history book — a bellows.

"He's a blacksmith!" Ryan exclaimed.

And then I saw two horses standing in a small stable behind the fire.

The man's biceps bulged as he pushed and pulled the bellows. With each push, it blew air onto the fire, making the flames jump.

He didn't see us until we stood a few feet away. I could feel the heat of the fire on my skin. I took a step back and pulled Ryan back with me.

The man's eyes went wide behind his tangles of hair. He gazed at us in surprise. His eyes traveled up and down as he studied us.

Finally, he spoke in a gruff voice: "Is the Prince having a costume ball?"

I didn't know how to answer that question. Prince? Costume ball? What was he talking about? Why was he staring at Ryan and me like we were Martians or something?

"We . . . we're lost," I finally blurted out. "Can you tell us where we are?"

He tossed back his head and laughed.

"No. Really," Ryan said. "Where are we?"

The blacksmith pointed to the far-off building. "Doesn't the castle give you a clue?"

The fire crackled. He picked up a huge pair of tongs and began heating them in the flames.

"You cannot be lost if the castle is in front of you," he said.

My mind spun with questions. "What year is this?" I blurted out.

He squinted at me. "I am but a blacksmith," he said. "How would I know the year?"

"But . . . we don't have blacksmiths anymore," I said. "We —"

"Where do you come from?" he asked. Flames licked at his hands. It didn't seem to bother him.

"From Tampa," Ryan answered.

The blacksmith turned away from the fire. He studied us again. "Does the Prince of Tampa know you have fled his kingdom?"

"Kingdom?" I said. "You don't understand. Tampa is a city. In Florida. We live near the bay."

He frowned. I could see he didn't like that answer.

He set the tongs down on the forge. He brushed back his hair. His dark eyes grew cold.

"Are you the ones the guards have been searching for?" he boomed.

"N-no," I stammered. "We just got here. We —"

He took a step toward us. My heart started to pound. He suddenly looked so big and menacing.

"Stay right there," he ordered. "Do not make any attempt to escape."

Escape?

He rumbled across the yellow dirt, waving his arms in front of him. "Guards! Guards!" he shouted. "Call for the guards!"

10

"Guards! Call for the guards!"

I could hear the blacksmith's booming voice behind us as we ran. Our sneakers kicked up the yellow dirt.

The two horses whinnied. We ran past the stable, along the row of open shacks.

Heads poked out from the little huts. Two shaggy-haired kids pointed and shouted at us as we darted past. A woman carrying a small brown dog stood in her doorway, her eyes bulging.

Ryan and I tore past a wooden cart brimming with hay. A man sat up drowsily in the hay as we went by.

Two women dressed in layers of rags, with long scraggly hair falling from their gray scarves, jumped back when they saw us. They hugged each other, terrified.

"Guards! Guards!"

I could still hear the blacksmith's alarmed shouts.

Why was he calling the guards on us? Who did he think we were?

"The wall — it goes on forever," Ryan said breathlessly. "There's no way out of here."

"We need a place to hide," I said, panting hard.

And then I let out a startled cry as I tripped over something in the dirt.

I fell hard and landed on my elbows and knees. "*Owwww.*" Pain shot up my body.

Ryan pulled me to my feet.

I turned and picked up the object I had tripped over. "Ryan — check it out," I said. Holding the handle with both hands, I raised the heavy blade in front of him.

"Remember? We saw this during our class trip to the museum? It's a battle-ax."

"Huh?" Ryan stared at it. "You mean like knights used in battle?"

I didn't have a chance to answer him. A net dropped over us. A metal mesh net, so heavy it slammed us both to our knees.

Through the net, I saw uniforms. Long black coats. Black trousers with red stripes down the side. Shiny black boots.

A group of guards.

"Let us go!" Ryan screamed. He thrashed both arms at the net, but it was too heavy to budge.

"Let us out of here!" I cried.

One of the guards leaned close to the net. He wore a black-and-red scarf under his long coat. A square red hat tilted on his head. He waved a sword in one hand.

He had cold gray eyes and a triumphant smile on his face.

"Captured!" he cried to the others. "We have captured the two villains! And look, guards — they still have the weapon they used to kill the Prince!"

"This isn't happening," Ryan muttered. "Did we step into an old movie or something?"

"It's like we went back in time!" I whispered. "But . . . that's *impossible* — right?"

I always get dizzy when I'm afraid. And believe me, the whole room was spinning.

The guards had dragged us into the castle. And now we were standing in an enormous chamber. It looked like it belonged in a video game about battling knights.

The gray stone walls rose high around us. They were covered with old-fashioned weapons. Round metal shields lined one wall. Long, pointed lances hung crisscrossed above them.

A shiny suit of armor stood at one tall doorway. It gripped a battle-ax in its metal glove. Up near the ceiling on one of the walls, a row of black-and-red flags jutted out on long poles. Dozens of swords with wide metal blades leaned against another wall draped with dark red curtains.

Flickering wall torches made the light dance over us. The guards surrounding us kept disappearing into the shadows. Then they would reappear in the firelight, their faces hard and cold under their square hats.

A black-uniformed guard in high red boots strode across the room to greet us. He gripped a sword at his side.

Wavy red hair poked out over his forehead. He had tiny round green eyes and a clipped red mustache.

"So the young assassins have been captured!" he cried. His voice echoed off the high stone walls.

"We're not assassins," I managed to choke out. My voice trembled. So did my legs. "We didn't kill anyone!"

He stared hard at Ryan, then at me. "Are those strange costumes supposed to frighten us? To confuse us?"

Strange costumes? I was wearing school clothes — a blue T-shirt and white cargo shorts. Ryan wore faded jeans and a black polo shirt.

"Why didn't you flee the castle when you had a chance?" the guard asked, still eyeing us up and down. "Do you not value your heads?"

I gasped. Ryan made a gulping sound.

"We're not assassins," I repeated. "You're making a big mistake. We didn't kill anyone! You've got to believe us!"

"We don't know where we are!" Ryan declared. "Really. We don't know who you are! We don't know anything about this!"

The guard tossed back his head and laughed. "Do you take me for a fool?" he said. "Were you not captured with your weapon in hand?"

"No! It wasn't ours!" I cried. "We found it in the dirt!"

His smile grew wider beneath the thin red mustache. "I promise you will confess to your crime before the day is over."

"This isn't going well," I whispered to Ryan.

"We need a good escape trick," Ryan muttered. He was trying to sound brave. But his face had turned pale, and I could see his chin quivering.

"Do not speak of escape," the guard said. "You will not be leaving this castle with your heads."

He waved his men forward. "This way," he ordered. "To their doom."

12

The torches along the wall flickered and danced as we marched under them. In the dim light, I saw a scrawny rat scamper under the heavy red drapes. Chill after chill rolled down my back. These men weren't kidding. They really believed Ryan and I were assassins.

It should be easy to prove that we're not killers, I thought. *But will they believe us? Will they even listen to us?*

The guards forced us into another chamber. A smaller room with dark green walls. A huge chandelier hung down from the ceiling. It cast bright light from hundreds of candles.

Flames danced in a tall fireplace. Torches blazed along the walls.

Beneath the chandelier, two men were seated in tall chairs at a long table. They were eating lunch. Their food was piled high on round silver plates. They were drinking from tall metal goblets.

They stood up as we walked in. They both wore long purple robes. The tall one was completely bald. His head glowed under the bright candles. He had coffee-colored skin, dark eyes, a long, pointed nose, and a deep scar that ran down one side of his face.

"Bow your heads before the Duke of Earle," the guard ordered us.

I didn't think about it. I bowed my head.

The man beside the Duke had the hood of his robe pulled over his head. His long white Santa beard came halfway down his chest. His dark eyes studied us. His hands were clasped tightly in front of him.

"Bow your heads to Henway, the Prince's Wizard," the guard ordered.

Ryan and I bowed our heads again.

Henway's hood fell back. He had flowing white hair to match his beard.

The Duke turned to the Wizard. "I shall bet you the girl confesses first," he said. "Would you like to bet five dumas?"

Henway frowned and shook his head. "No more betting, Alfred," he said sharply. "Your constant gambling has gotten you into much trouble before. Alfred, have you not learned your lesson?"

The Duke shrugged. "An innocent bet. To pass the time."

"You have the betting sickness," Henway scolded.

The Duke smiled at that. "Not a sickness. An enjoyable game."

Henway made a disgusted sound. He stepped up close to Ryan and me. His robe smelled bad, as if it had never been washed. He rubbed a hand through his thick beard and stared at us.

Henway waved the guards back. They retreated to the doorway and stood there stiffly alert.

"You assassins will be brought to a quick justice," he said.

"But you're wrong!" I cried. "We are not assassins!"

The Duke snickered. "Then why have you disguised yourselves in those strange costumes?" he demanded.

"S-strange costumes?" I stammered.

"This is what we wear to school every day," Ryan said.

Both men snickered at that. They exchanged glances.

"We're telling the truth!" I cried. My voice came out high and shrill.

"Why did you sneak onto the castle grounds?" the Duke asked.

"We didn't sneak," I said. "We —"

"We don't know how we got here!" Ryan exclaimed.

Henway scratched his beard. The Duke laughed. "Surely you can come up with a better answer than that!" he said. "Why don't you say you arrived on a cloud? Or rode on the back of a dragon?"

They both laughed at that.

"How did you get here? Tell us," the Duke insisted.

"Really!" I cried. "We don't know!"

"Where do you come from?" Henway asked.

"Tampa," Ryan and I said together.

"A fantasy kingdom!" Henway said. "The Prince has a whole library of maps. And in all those maps there is no Kingdom of Tampa."

"Can you not give an honest answer to a single question?" the Duke demanded.

"Must I conjure a spell to draw the truth from you?" Henway asked.

Ryan turned to me. "I think we're in major trouble here," he whispered.

Ryan was right. They didn't believe a word we said. Every answer we gave dug us deeper into trouble.

I took a deep breath. "Something strange has happened," I told them. "Ryan and I come from a different time. I — I think we've gone back in time."

The room began to spin. I felt dizzy again. I realized I was terrified. Was I really talking about time travel?

"We really don't know how we got here," Ryan said. "But . . . look at us. We're just kids. *No way* we are assassins! We didn't kill anybody!"

"More lies," the Duke said softly.

"Very clever lies," Henway said. "But lies just the same."

"Very clever disguises, too," the Duke said. "They really do look like children."

He rubbed the scar on the side of his face, thinking hard. Then he turned back to the Wizard. "Would you care to bet on how old they really are? Three dumas?"

Henway waved the Duke away. "No betting, Alfred. Please try to control yourself."

Henway turned away from the Duke and frowned at us. His dark eyes went cloudy. "Your violent act has tossed the kingdom into sorrow and chaos," he said. "Prince Warwick shall have his revenge!"

Huddled close to me, Ryan made another gulping sound. My whole body suddenly went cold all over.

No one likes to hear the word *revenge*.

My mind spun with ideas. I thought about my dad's best escape trick. No way it could help Ryan and me. You need a tall mirror to do it.

I struggled to think of a way to explain to them what had happened. But what would make them believe us?

One last try. "I . . . I picked up the battle-ax

from the ground," I stammered. "Actually, I tripped over it. I was running, and I tripped over it."

"That's right," Ryan chimed in. "We were both running, and Jessica tripped over that weapon. I saw her pick it up and —"

"Why were you running?" Henway asked.

"Because you are guilty," the Duke answered for us. "And you were trying to escape."

"You will not escape your fate," Henway said, lowering his voice.

"Would you like to make a small bet with me?" the Duke asked. "I bet that Prince Warwick will have your heads off before nightfall."

"No. Please —" I cried.

They motioned the guards forward. The guards moved quickly and grabbed our arms, holding us tightly.

Henway and the Duke of Earle turned, walked through a door, and led the way into a long, dark hallway. The guards forced us to follow.

"Wh-where are you taking us?" I demanded.

"To see your victim, the Prince," Henway replied.

"I don't understand," I said in a trembling voice. My legs were shaking so hard, I could barely walk. "Our victim? The Prince? What do you mean?"

They didn't answer. The guards pulled us forward.

Our shoes scuffled across the hard floor. Flickering light danced over us from a long row of wall torches. Enormous paintings lined the walls.

Dreary portraits of grim-looking kings and queens wearing gray crowns and dark fur robes. Their expressions were all stern and cold. None of them smiled.

At the end of the hall, the Duke and the Wizard stepped aside as the guards pushed open a door. Then the two men led the way into a bright chamber.

The sudden light made me blink. When my eyes adjusted, I gazed around quickly. The walls appeared to be made of gold! Sunlight flooded in through tall windows. Golden drapes hung at their sides. Dark, heavy furniture filled the center of the room.

"Here we are, Prince Warwick," the Duke announced.

Against the back wall, a man sat at a long writing table. My gaze stopped at the writing quill in his hand.

And then I raised my eyes. And Ryan and I both opened our mouths in screams of horror.

The Prince had only a lumpy stub on his shoulders. He was HEADLESS!

13

My knees buckled. I started to fall.

But two guards held me up.

Beside me, Ryan screamed again. "No! It's IMPOSSIBLE!"

I wanted to look away. But I couldn't take my eyes off the headless man.

He wore a ruffled white shirt. The collar was pinned shut. Above the collar, the stub of his neck was pink. A dark scab had formed over the top.

I shut my eyes. I felt my stomach lurch. I struggled to hold down my breakfast.

"He has no head, but he's alive. This has to be a fake," Ryan whispered. "Some kind of magic trick."

I lowered my eyes to the ruffled shirt. Was the neck stub a fake? Was he hiding his head under the shirt?

No.

"It . . . it's real," I choked out. I swallowed again and again. My stomach churned.

If only I could look away from that dark ugly scab.

The Duke and Henway stepped up to the Prince. I tried to stay back, but the guards pushed Ryan and me closer.

"The Prince's magic is more powerful than your ax," Henway said to me. "He learned magic from me. Studied his entire life. And his magic is more powerful than anyone dreamed. His magic allows him to live on even though you chopped off his head."

"But — but —" I sputtered. I felt sick. The room tilted and spun.

"Your Excellency," the Duke said, sweeping back his robe to take a deep bow. "I am pleased to report that we have captured the two assassins."

"They were caught with the weapon in their hands," Henway added.

The headless Prince froze for a long moment. Then he raised his ruffled sleeve and began to write furiously on the parchment in front of him.

The quill made a scratchy sound as he wrote, leaning over the table. When he finished writing, he lowered the quill. Then he raised the parchment so we could read what he had written:

WHERE IS MY HEAD?

"We don't know!" I cried in a high, shrill voice. The words just blurted out. "We don't know anything about this! Please — believe us!"

"We don't belong here!" Ryan said. "We don't even know where we are!"

We were screaming at a headless man!

He shook the sheet of parchment in one hand. Then he pointed to his words again:

WHERE IS MY HEAD?

"We don't know! Really!" I cried.

He jabbed his finger at the parchment again. And again.

WHERE IS MY HEAD?

Then he lowered the parchment to the table and began to write again. His hand moved quickly across the page. When he finished it, he raised it for us to read:

WHY DID YOU TAKE MY HEAD?

I was too frightened to reply. I knew I'd be seeing that horrible stump in my dreams. If I lived long enough to have dreams!

I turned to Ryan. His eyes were covered by his sunglasses. But I could still see the fear on his face. He couldn't speak, either.

"Will you not answer Prince Warwick's question?" Henway demanded.

The Duke played with the scar down the side of his face. "I'd be willing to bet that I could get them to talk," he said.

He turned to the Prince. "Sometimes pain will loosen the tongue. Perhaps, Your Excellency, they will answer your question after a few hours in the torture chamber!"

"Ohhh!" A terrified moan escaped my throat.

The Prince shook his whole body as if saying no.

Then he began to write furiously once again. A few seconds later, he held up what he had written:

DO NOT WASTE TIME. TAKE THEM TO THE EXECUTIONER. BRING ME THEIR HEADS WHEN HE HAS FINISHED.

"No — please!" Ryan choked out in a hoarse voice. "Please — believe us! We're telling you the truth!"

"We don't know anything!" I cried. "Please —"

I jerked one arm loose from the guard's strong grip. Then I twisted my body hard, trying to free myself from the guard at my other side.

But he held on tight. Both guards tightened their grips on my shoulders.

I couldn't move.

I turned to the Duke and the Wizard. "You have to help us. You have the wrong people. You're making a big mistake."

Henway frowned at us and brushed a hand through his white beard. "YOU made the mistake," he said softly.

The Duke bowed to the headless Prince again. "We must follow our Prince's command," he said. "We are his loyal servants."

“Prince Warwick is only being fair,” Henway said. “A head for a head. Can you argue with that?”

“Yes!” I said.

I started to say more. But a guard clapped his hand over my mouth. And spun me around.

What happened next was a blur of long, dark halls . . . grim portraits of frowning royalty . . . dizzying twists and turns . . . flickering torchlight. . . .

. . . And the thumping . . . thumping . . . thumping of my heartbeats. Every muscle in my body tightened with fear. My eyes blurred. Red spots darted in front of me. My legs felt rubbery and weak.

I knew Ryan was close beside me. But I was too terrified to look at him or to speak to him. Too terrified to *think*!

And then there we were. Outdoors. I felt the heat of the late afternoon sun.

Where had they dragged us? I gazed around at gray stone walls. We were on a roof. Maybe a roof of one of the castle towers. We were walled in on all four sides. The surface of the roof was black and sticky like tar.

Guards in black-and-red uniforms stood stiffly against the wall. They rested the points of their lances on the floor and carried round metal shields in front of them.

I saw a wooden platform, about two feet tall, I guessed.

The Duke and the Wizard stepped up to the platform. The wind ruffled their purple robes. The Duke's bald head gleamed in the sunlight.

And then a man stepped out from behind a low wall. I knew who he was just by looking at him. He was big, with a broad, bare chest and huge biceps. His legs were as thick as tree trunks, covered in ragged black pants that came down to his worn black boots. He wore a black mask over his head. I could see dark eyes behind the eye slits. He had a long-handled ax gripped tightly in one of his huge hands.

He was the executioner.

And the platform was the chopping block.

Ryan pushed up close to me. I could see the goose bumps on his arms. His whole body shuddered. "That guy . . . he looks like a comic-book executioner," he whispered.

"But . . . this isn't a comic book," I choked out.

I stared at the ax as the executioner swung it onto his massive shoulder. The broad blade caught the sunlight and glowed as if on fire.

"The girl will go first," the Duke of Earle said with a wave of his hand. "Do you have any last words?"

"Last words?" Hot tears ran down my cheeks. "H-here are my last words," I stammered. "Ryan and I have been telling the truth. My name is

Jessica Bowen, and he is Ryan Chang. We come from a city called Tampa, Florida. I'm not sure, but I think we live in the future. We are just kids. We do not belong here. We —"

"Enough!" Henway shouted. "We do not have time for fairy tales! Your stories do not convince us, girl!"

He gave the executioner a wave. "Chop off her head. Let justice be served."

Two guards pushed me to my knees. Then they forced my head over the chopping block.

"Please —" I gasped.

"This will teach you a lesson," Henway said.

I could see only the hem of his robe. And the boots of the guards. And the tar on the roof where my head would soon roll.

I felt a whir of hot air. A shadow swept over me as the executioner raised his ax high.

I shut my eyes. I held my breath.

Can this really be happening to me? I asked myself.

Above me, I heard the executioner groan as he prepared to swing the ax down.

Suddenly, I had a desperate idea.

15

"One last word!" I screamed. "Give me one last word!"

The shadow of the ax swept over me again as the executioner lowered it to his side.

The guards loosened their hold. I lifted my head from the chopping block.

My heart pounded like thunder inside my chest. My head throbbed.

Could I really *do* this?

Henway gazed down at me. "Do you have a final word of apology for your crime?" he demanded.

I turned to the Duke. His purple robe flapped in the wind. He frowned down at me, hands folded in front of him.

"Did you say you like to bet?" I asked him.

He nodded. "Well . . . yes. I have been known to make a wager from time to time."

I glanced at Ryan. Did he catch on to my plan?

I couldn't see his face. He was surrounded by guards.

"There will be no gambling while we are carrying out the Prince's orders," Henway said sternly. "Alfred, you have been warned about your gambling again and again."

I ignored him and kept my eyes on the Duke. He stepped closer. I could see that I had grabbed his interest.

"Have you ever bet on a coin toss?" I asked him.

A thin smile played over his lips. "Perhaps," he replied.

I took a deep breath.

Could this plan actually work?

I knew I'd have to use my best acting skills.

"I enjoy betting, too," I said. "Would you like to bet on a coin toss?"

The Wizard grabbed the Duke's sleeve. "Alfred — stop this at once!" he snapped.

The Duke stepped closer. He pulled me to my feet. His eyes gazed into mine.

"A coin toss?" he said softly. "I can never resist a coin toss. But I should warn you, I seldom lose."

"The Prince will not approve," Henway scolded. "Your endless gambling must stop!"

The Duke gave him a gentle push out of the way. "And what is the nature of this bet?" he asked me, eyes flashing.

"Simple," I replied. "If you win the toss, carry out the execution. Chop off our heads."

He rubbed his chin. "And if *you* win the toss?"

"Then you will spare our lives," I said.

"Enough of this!" Henway barked. "Stop this at once, Alfred! I shall not allow it!"

The Duke's smile grew wider. "It sounds like a fair bet. I will agree to it," he said. "But you must know that I will win. I am very lucky. You are delaying your fate for only a few moments."

My hand trembled as I reached into my shorts pocket. My fingers were shaking so hard, I nearly dropped the gold coin.

I held the coin up in front of the Duke. "Shall I toss it?" I asked.

He nodded. "Proceed."

I took a deep breath. Then I flipped the coin into the air. "Heads, I win!" I cried.

We all watched it come down. It bounced once on the roof, then stuck in the tar surface.

The Duke leaned down to see the result. He uttered a groan. "Heads. You win, girl." He pounded his fists against the sides of his legs. "How is this possible? I never lose!"

He made a grab for the coin. But I picked it up first and stuffed it back in my pocket before he could examine it. Then I pumped my fists in the air. "We win!"

"We win! We win!" Ryan cried, jumping up and down.

But our celebration didn't last long.

Henway scowled at the Duke and brushed him out of the way. "I am sorry," the Wizard said, his cold eyes locked on mine. "But I cannot allow the Duke's foolish wager to stand."

He motioned to the big man beside the chopping block. "Executioner, prepare your ax!"

16

"No!" I shouted.

The Duke turned angrily to the Wizard and stuck out his chest. "A wager is a wager," he said.

Henway shook his head. "It was an improper wager."

"I do not care," the Duke shot back. "My honor is at stake! I must keep my word."

Henway ran a hand through his thick white hair.

I had my fingers crossed tightly. Who was going to win this argument?

Henway let out a disgusted sigh. "Very well. Be a fool," he snapped at the Duke. "Spare their lives."

Yes! We win! I thought.

But then Henway added: "Take them to the castle dungeon. After a few days down there, they will *beg* us to chop off their heads!"

Huh? Ryan and I exchanged glances. The

dungeon? I could feel my heart drop into my stomach. A frightened cry escaped my throat.

A few seconds later, the sunlight disappeared behind us. We were forced down deep, dark stairways. The stones were damp and covered with slimy green moss.

Ryan and I kept slipping on the hard, slick stairs. The guards held on to us to keep us from falling.

The air grew cold and sour. Chill after chill shook my body.

Deeper into the castle. The only sound was our shoes and the guards' boots thudding on the slippery stones.

Henway had gone off by himself. But the Duke followed us down. He rattled the dungeon keys in his robe as we made our way.

Finally, we stepped out into a low chamber. I squinted, trying to see. The room was lit by only a few flickering candles. Our shoes scraped over crackling, dry straw.

I stared into the deep shadows. And heard the groans and moans of dungeon prisoners.

"Hungry! Hungry! Hungry!" a hoarse voice repeated. "Did you bring any num-nums? Any num-nums?"

I heard a scratching sound in the straw at my feet. I jumped as something scrambled over my shoe.

A rat?

I squeezed Ryan's arm. His whole body was trembling.

The guards forced us through a curtain of thick cobwebs. I brushed the sticky webbing from my face.

And saw an endless row of cells. They marched us down the row. I stared straight ahead. I couldn't bear to see the ragged men in their cages, sprawled on the floor or clinging to the bars.

My whole body shook as they forced us to the last cage at the very end. The cell bars were rusted black. The floor had thick, matted piles of straw. Even from outside, I could see fat black insects crawling in the straw.

The air felt thick and heavy. I could hear the buzzing of flies.

The Duke handed the keys to a guard. The guard turned a key in the lock and pulled open the cell door. The door squeaked as it slid open.

The guards gave Ryan and me a hard push into the cell. Ryan tumbled into the wooden bench. I fell facedown into the straw.

"Ohhh, sick!" I groaned as prickly bugs crawled over my face.

I jumped to my feet, slapping at my cheeks. I brushed bugs off the front of my T-shirt. My whole body started to itch.

The cell door slammed. I turned and watched the Duke leading the guards away.

"Hey — come back!" Ryan shouted. He grabbed the bars at the front of the cell and poked his face out. "Come back! How long do we have to stay in here?"

"You won your bet. We spared your lives. Why are you complaining?" the Duke called. Then he disappeared into the darkness.

All around us, men howled and shouted. In the corner of our cell, I saw the skeleton of a small animal. Bugs swarmed over the bones.

"Hungry! Johnny is hungry!" a man moaned from somewhere down the long row of cells. "Johnny is hungry. Who will feed Johnny?"

"We — we can't stay here," I stammered. "We have to get out."

Ryan nodded but didn't say anything. He hugged himself, trying to stop the shakes.

"This is too weird," I murmured. "We have to think of something."

Suddenly, a face appeared in the cell next to ours. A pale, bald man with gray eyes sunken deep in their sockets. He opened his mouth, and I saw that he had no teeth. "I am innocent," he said in a horrible, raspy whisper like chalk on a chalkboard. "My name is Innocent. My mother named me Innocent. So how can I be guilty?"

Ryan and I stared at him. We didn't know how to reply. He waved a bony hand like a limp white fish. "Did you bring me a treat? Can I have my treat now?"

"Sorry. No treat," I said. I pressed my fingers over my nose. The man smelled like rotten meat.

"But . . . my name is Innocent!" he rasped. Then he spotted a fat black spider on the dungeon floor. He grabbed it and popped it into his mouth. "Thanks for the treat," he said. He sank back into the shadows of his cell.

I shivered. Ryan was still hugging himself. I could see my reflection in his silver glasses. My hair was totally messed up. I had a smear of dirt down one cheek.

"We have to think hard," I said. "Some kind of magic brought us to this awful place. Maybe some kind of magic can help us escape."

Ryan nodded. "Maybe . . ." he said in a tiny voice.

"The coin," I said. "It was the two-headed coin."

Down the row, a man began to sing. His voice kept cracking. His song had no melody. And the words made no sense.

The singing made other prisoners shout and howl. One prisoner meowed like a cat. The noise echoed off the low ceilings.

"The coin brought us here," I said. I had to shout over the deafening howls. "Don't you remember?"

Ryan blinked. "You're right, Jessica. It was in

the grass. On the playground. And we both grabbed for it at the same time."

"Yes," I said. "Our hands both wrapped around the coin, and . . . and then we began to flip over and over."

"So maybe if we both grab the coin again . . ." Ryan said.

My heart began to race with excitement. Maybe it would work. Maybe the coin would flip us out of here. Back to the playground, where we'd started.

I grabbed the coin in my pocket and pulled it out. Holding it between my fingers, I raised it in front of us.

"Okay. Grab it on the count of three," I told Ryan. "Are you ready? One . . . two . . ."

But my hand was shaking so hard, the coin slipped out.

"Nooo!" I screamed as it fell. I swiped at it wildly.

Missed.

The coin bounced onto the floor and rolled into the thick straw.

"Oh, no. Oh, no," I muttered.

Ryan and I dropped to our knees. I began sifting through the straw with both hands.

Where was it? *Where?*

"It's too dark," Ryan moaned. "I can't see anything."

"Keep searching," I said. I swatted a fat bug off the back of my hand.

Frantically, I brushed the straw floor. I turned and searched behind me.

I searched until I'd made a complete circle. Searched with both hands, brushing and scraping straw out of the way.

"It couldn't roll far," I murmured. "It *couldn't*!"

Finally, Ryan sat up. He pulled off his sunglasses. I could see the fear on his face.

"Jessica, we lost it," he whispered. "We lost the coin."

17

Ryan helped pull me to my feet. I brushed off my legs. I pulled a bug off the front of my shorts.

I shut my eyes. I wanted to cry. I wanted to scream.

I wanted to howl like the other sad dungeon prisoners.

When I opened my eyes, Ryan had a smile on his face. I blinked a few times. Was I seeing things?

"What?" I said. "You're smiling?"

He pointed down to the floor. I lowered my gaze. He was pointing at my left sneaker.

I cried out when I saw the gold coin caught in the laces.

"It didn't hit the floor," Ryan said. "It landed on your shoe."

I let out a long sigh of relief. Then I grabbed the coin. I held it tightly in my fist. "You're not getting away again," I told it.

Did the coin have the magic to take us out of this dungeon?

All around us, prisoners began to shout and cheer. They banged on their cell bars until the noise was so loud, I covered my ears.

I saw a ragged man with long, stringy white hair moving from cell to cell. He stepped up to our cell door. He carried a flat wooden tray stacked with metal bowls.

He set it down and pulled out a small ring of keys. He put one of the keys in the door and opened our cell. Just wide enough to shove in two bowls filled with gray muck. It looked like wet plaster.

"Feed time," the man muttered. "My last stop."

Ryan stepped to the door to pick up the bowls. "What are we having for lunch?" he asked the man.

The man squinted at Ryan. "Lunch? What is lunch?" he asked. "Did you find that word in a book?"

Ryan just shook his head. "Don't we get spoons?"

The man rolled his eyes. "Crazy prisoners," he muttered. "Spoons? Making up your own words?" He slammed the cell door shut.

We watched him walk away, swinging the tray at his side.

Ryan set the two bowls down on the wooden

bench. The soup or whatever it was smelled like sour buttermilk.

Was this our only meal of the day?

I felt sick. I grabbed my stomach.

When I turned to Ryan, he was grinning again.

"What's up *this* time?" I demanded.

His grin grew wider. He reached behind his back and pulled something out of his pocket.

I gaped at it in amazement.

The food man's keys!

Despite my fear, I burst out laughing. I slapped Ryan on the back. "Wow! You haven't lost your touch!"

"When you're good, you're good," Ryan said.

He raised the keys and we both stepped to the cell door.

"Let's get out of here," I said.

I didn't realize how hard that would be.

18

The keys clattered on the key ring. Ryan leaned against the bars and fumbled a key into the lock. He tried to turn it.

"No," he said. "Wrong key."

There were at least ten keys on the ring.

Ryan took the key out. The space between the bars was narrow. His hand barely fit through.

He tried the next key. Then the next.

My heart pounded harder with each try. "One of them has to work," I said. "We saw that guard open the door."

The cell door popped open on the next try. "Yesss!" Ryan whispered.

I glanced at the man in the next cell. Was he watching? No. He was flat on his back, sound asleep. We were in the very last cell. No one else could see us.

I slowly pushed the rusted door open. It squeaked as it swept across the straw floor.

"Good work, Ryan," I said. "Let's go!"

I didn't think about *where* we would go. I just wanted to leave that horrible cell.

We both hurried out. Ryan tossed the keys back into the cell and slammed the door shut.

"Which way?" he asked.

I glanced from one side to the other. In the dim light, I could see only the endless row of cells.

"We've got to find the stairs," I said. "The first thing is to get away from this dungeon."

Ryan pointed to the left. "I think we came that way."

We started to run. Our shoes scraped the straw. I squinted hard into the darkness, trying to find the stairway.

Prisoners shouted at us and howled.

"Let us out!" someone yelled. "Set us free!"

"Freedom! I want freedom!"

"Johnny is hungry! Johnny is hungry!"

We ran until we reached a wide aisle. I saw a break in the row of cells.

Ryan turned. "Let's try this way," he said breathlessly.

We took off — then stopped.

I heard heavy footsteps. The thud of boots on the floor. A man coughed loudly, a booming cough that echoed off the walls.

I grabbed Ryan and pulled him behind a cell. "It's a guard. He . . . he's coming this way!"

"He'll see us!" Ryan gasped.

“Hurry,” I said. “Back to our cell. We’ll wait for him to leave.”

We both spun around, our shoes slipping in the straw.

The other prisoners shouted and howled and begged as we hurtled back to our cell.

“Freedom! I demand freedom!”

“Let us out! Let us out!”

“Johnny is hungry!”

I glanced over my shoulder. The guard was taking long strides, heading our way. His sword swung against his leg. He wore a loose black cape that flapped behind him as he walked.

We both were gasping for breath by the time we made it back to the cell.

My head throbbed and my throat ached.

“Hurry — he’s coming!” Ryan’s voice cracked. “Get back in the cell before he sees us!”

I grabbed the bars and pulled. The door didn’t budge.

“It — it’s *locked*,” I gasped.

Ryan grabbed the door. He pulled hard. Then he pushed it.

No way. The door was locked.

I stared into the cell. Stared at the keys on the straw floor where Ryan had tossed them.

We were locked out.

Trapped.

The guard was moving fast, swinging his arms as he walked. He had a sour look on his face. His eyes were locked straight ahead.

I pressed my back against the bars. I pulled Ryan beside me. We tried to flatten ourselves against the cell. Maybe if he kept staring straight ahead, he wouldn't come all the way down the hallway.

I held my breath as he strode closer, down the long row of cells.

Suddenly, he stopped. His eyes bulged in surprise. "You there!" he shouted.

I let out a gasp. "He sees us!"

Too late to run.

The guard gripped his sword handle as he began to charge toward us. He narrowed his eyes at us, and his expression turned angry. "You there! Do not move!"

I felt Ryan tremble beside me. My throat tightened in fear. I struggled to breathe.

The guard drew his sword. He raised it in front of him. His cape billowed behind him.

"Prisoners! You have been captured!" he boomed.

"We're . . . doomed," Ryan whispered, pressed against the bars.

The guard stopped a few yards in front of us. He was a big man, way over six feet tall. Powerful looking with broad shoulders and a huge chest under his uniform jacket.

He swung the sword in front of him. The blade glimmered in the flickering candlelight.

And a girl's voice behind him called out: "*Hey, you jerk! Watch where you're going!*"

Startled, he dropped the sword. It clattered to the floor. He spun away from us. "Who goes there?"

I gave Ryan a shove. "Move!"

I pushed myself from the cell bars and took off running. We ran side by side down the long aisle of dungeon cells.

I glanced back. The guard stooped to pick up his sword. He still had a confused look on his face.

Prisoners hooted and howled. They banged the bars of their cells and screamed at the guard.

"This way!" I cried to Ryan. We spun around a corner and headed down a narrow passageway. "Maybe we can lose him."

"Who was that girl?" Ryan asked, running hard to keep up with me.

"Who do you think?" I replied.

"It was YOU?" he cried.

"Of course it was me," I said. "All that practice throwing my voice paid off."

The passage narrowed until it became a low tunnel. It was barely wide enough for us to squeeze through, and so low we had to stoop.

I lowered my head and kept moving through total darkness now. I could hear Ryan close behind me.

I stopped to listen for the guard's footsteps — and Ryan came crashing into me.

"Ow!" I cried out as we both toppled to the tunnel floor. I landed hard on my elbows and knees.

The floor was wet and mucky.

Was this some kind of sewer?

"Jessica — sorry. I —" Ryan started to climb to his feet.

"Shhh." I held my breath and listened.

Silence.

I could hear my heart beat over my wheezing breath.

No guard.

"I think we lost him," I whispered. My voice sounded hollow in the narrow tunnel.

"But . . . where are we?" Ryan asked. "I can't see a thing. Where does this lead?"

"We escaped from the dungeon," I said. "Now let's just keep going and see where we come out."

"But, Jessica —"

"We don't have a choice, right?"

"Right," he replied. "We can't go back. There are probably a hundred guards looking for us now."

I lowered my head again and pressed my hands against the tunnel walls as I led the way through the darkness. The tunnel twisted and curved, and I could feel the floor tilt as we headed up.

"It has to lead somewhere," I murmured to Ryan. And then I saw a patch of gray up ahead. Just a small square of brightness in the distance.

"The end of the tunnel!" I cried.

It glimmered like a light. I ducked my head and ran toward it.

Was that the sky?

We can do this, I told myself. *We can find the end of this long black tunnel.*

But then I let out a moan as my hopes all faded.

I staggered to a stop.

I sobbed.

And stared at the tall guard standing in the center of the tunnel opening. Watching us, waiting for us, blocking our escape.

Behind me, Ryan gasped. He dropped wearily to his knees.

We were too exhausted to turn around and run back. Besides, there were probably guards waiting for us at the other end.

We had no choice.

"Okay," I called to the guard. "We give up." I raised both hands above my head in surrender.

"We give up. You've caught us!"

20

The guard didn't move.

"We're coming out," I called. "Please — don't hurt us. We are surrendering."

He stood still. Eyes staring. Back rigid with his hand on his sword, waiting for us.

"Weird," Ryan muttered. "What's up with this guy?"

I stepped out of the tunnel into a large chamber. I stood up straight and stretched my arms above my head. I had been walking stooped over for so long, my back and shoulders ached.

I kept my eyes on the guard, standing so stiffly in the gray light up ahead. "Sir?"

Ryan came flying out of the tunnel. Then he froze, staring at me beside the guard.

"Sir?" I took a step closer. Then I burst out laughing. "Ryan — he isn't real!"

We both stepped up to the guard. I made a fist and tapped his chest. "Wood," I said. "He's carved out of wood."

Ryan grabbed the sword handle. "It's wood, too." He pounded his fist into the guard's stomach. "Gotcha!"

I stared up at the stern carved face. "I guess he's here to scare people back into the dungeon," I said.

Ryan tapped the wooden boot with his shoe. "If I had my Swiss Army knife, I'd carve my initials in the wood!"

"Don't be dumb," I said. "We don't have time for that. All the Prince's guards must be searching for us by now. What are we going to do?"

"The coin," Ryan said. "Set it down on the floor. Hurry. Then we'll both grab it at the same time. Maybe it will send us back home."

I pulled the coin from my pocket. I bent down to set it on the stone floor. Then I gasped. "Footsteps. Someone is coming!"

I tucked the coin back in my shorts pocket. Then I gazed around the large chamber. Several doorways lined the walls.

I ran to the nearest door. Ryan followed close beside me. We peered into a small room. It held a ladder and a lot of brooms and buckets.

"A supply closet," I murmured. "No place to hide in here."

The next room was more interesting. It had shelves piled with red-and-black robes. "Quick," I said. I ran into the room and began pulling robes off the shelves. I was searching for one that fit me.

"What are you doing?" Ryan asked from the doorway.

"Find a robe," I said. "Hurry. Pull it over your clothes."

"I get it," Ryan said. "A quick-change act. They'll be looking for us in our shorts and T-shirts. So if we're in robes . . ."

"Maybe we can fool them," I said.

Ryan pulled a pile of robes off a shelf. They were all too long for him. Finally, he found a shorter one and lowered it over his head.

The robe had a rope belt. He pulled it tight and knotted it. He looked totally ridiculous with his silver sunglasses and his black sneakers poking out from under the old-fashioned robe.

I found one, too. The robe was very heavy and smelled stale. "Pull the hood over your head," I instructed Ryan.

He snickered. "And mess up my hair?"

"Get serious," I said. "This isn't a joke."

"Tell me about it," he said with a groan.

The hoods fit loosely. But they covered our faces pretty well.

We both listened. Silence out there now. No one coming.

We tried the coin again. I set it down on the floor, and we both grabbed it at the same time. Ryan's hand closed over mine. We waited.

Nothing happened.

"What are we doing wrong?" Ryan asked.

"Maybe we have to try it on the other side of the wall," I said. "The spot where we landed."

He frowned. "How do we get out of this place? We can't just walk out. The grounds are surrounded by walls. And the guards will be looking for us."

"Maybe we can steal those two horses from the blacksmith," I said.

Ryan shook his head. "No way. I don't want to mess with that guy. He's a giant!"

I thought hard. "First, we have to get out of this castle," I said. "That won't be easy."

Ryan scratched the front of his robe. "This thing is totally itchy," he muttered. Then his mouth dropped open. "Hey — here's an idea."

I stared at him. "Yes?"

"What if we help the Prince?"

"Help him?" I said. "How?"

"He wants his head back — right?" Ryan asked. "What if we help him find it? Then he'll be happy to let us go home — right?"

"But the head is probably far away by now," I argued. "The real assassins probably came on horses, took the Prince's head, and galloped away as fast as they could."

"No way," Ryan said. He began to pace back and forth, thinking hard. "They didn't come to the castle on horses. If they did, they would have been seen. They would have been stopped by the guards."

"You're right," I said. "So they probably came on foot, maybe late at night. And they sneaked into the castle."

"The assassins might still be around here," Ryan said. "Maybe they are having trouble escaping, like us."

I nodded. "That means Prince Warwick's head could still be around. Maybe they dumped it. You know. Hid it somewhere so they wouldn't be caught with it."

Ryan stopped pacing. "Jessica, if we find the Prince's head, we'll be *heroes*!"

We stepped out of the robe room. I gazed at the big wooden guard. I let out a sigh. "This castle is so big, Ryan," I said. "We could search for a year."

He tucked his hands into the deep robe pockets. "You're right," he murmured. He scrunched up his face. "Let's think. If I wanted to hide a head, where would I stash it?"

"It's hopeless," I said. "Hopeless. If we go running around the castle, searching for the head, we'll be caught in five minutes."

"Wait! I just thought of something," Ryan said. "The assassins wouldn't want the head to be found — right?"

"Right," I said.

"So they wouldn't hide it inside the castle with

people walking all around. They probably hid the head *outside* the castle."

"You're definitely right," I agreed. "We have to get out and search —"

I stopped because I heard voices. Very nearby. Men talking. Coming our way.

I whipped my head around. "Ryan — quick! How do we get out of here?"

21

The voices grew louder. I realized it was Henway and the Duke of Earle.

Ryan darted behind the wooden guard and tried to make himself small.

"That's not going to work," I whispered. "I can see your robe."

I had an idea. I ran back to the supply closet and grabbed the ladder.

I dragged it under the nearest window. With a groan, I propped it up against the wall.

"Good work!" Ryan cried.

I scrambled up first. My shoes slipped on the wooden rungs. I pulled myself halfway up to the window. Then I stopped. I had a horrifying thought. What if we were high off the ground?

"Jessica — hurry! They'll see us!" Ryan pleaded. He was right behind me.

I had no choice. I climbed to the top — and dove out the window.

THUD. I landed on my side and rolled in the dirt.

A short fall, only a few feet.

"Whew!" I let out a relieved sigh.

I turned and watched Ryan land hard on his hands and knees. He quickly scrambled away from the castle wall.

Behind us, I could hear the men's voices inside the castle.

Ryan pulled me to my feet, and we began to run.

Our shoes kicked up the yellow dirt. We lowered our heads and tore away from the castle.

And ran straight into a squad of marching guards.

22

We stopped so fast, we nearly knocked each other over.

My hood slipped off my head. I grabbed it and pulled it back into place.

The guards held swords in front of them. They marched in a double line. Their red hats caught the light of the late afternoon sun. Their eyes were fixed straight ahead.

"Walk normal," I whispered to Ryan.

He swallowed. "Huh? Normal?"

We pulled our hoods as low as we could. And we walked slowly, side by side. We walked toward the guards as if we had nothing to hide.

My legs felt as soft as noodles. I don't know how I forced them to move. My heart was beating so hard, I felt dizzy.

Ryan and I kept walking.

Closer . . . closer . . . until they were only a few feet from us!

Did they see us?

The guards didn't even look at us. They kept their eyes locked straight ahead and marched together in silence. I turned and watched them move toward the front of the castle.

Ryan and I leaned against a tree trunk and took a few minutes to catch our breath. I was sweating inside the robe. I scratched the back of my neck and gazed around. We stood at one side of the castle. Behind us, a round stone tower rose up above the trees. In front of us, I saw a row of low shacks with thatched roofs and boarded-up windows.

"If I assassinated the Prince, I'd hide his head in one of those shacks," I said. I squinted hard at Ryan. "Still want to be a hero?"

He returned my stare. "Yes. If it will get us out of here."

"Let's start searching the shacks," I said, "and see if we come up with anything."

Leaning against the tree, I gazed all around. No more guards in sight. I motioned Ryan forward, and we made our way across the dirt to the first shack. The door was missing. We peered inside. Empty. A flat dirt floor with nothing on it.

In the next shack, we saw two children crawling around in a pile of rags. Where were their parents?

"We've got to keep searching," I said.

We made our way to the next low building. I sniffed the air. The shack smelled of animals.

I pressed my face against the door and listened. Silence inside.

It was built of boards and wood scraps slapped carelessly together. There were holes up and down the front wall. The door was a single plank of wood.

"I think it's empty," I whispered to Ryan. I grabbed the side of the door and pushed it open.

Dark inside. I waited for my eyes to adjust. "Anyone in here?" My voice came out in a trembling whisper.

I froze in place and listened. I heard a scratching sound. A pattering. Like little feet running across the floor.

Ryan grabbed my shoulder. "Look, Jessica — the floor is covered in straw."

I squinted into the dim grayness. Yes. I saw mounds of straw — several piles — across the floor.

"Weird," I muttered. "Who would make piles of straw inside their house?"

"A good place to hide a head," Ryan whispered. He grabbed my shoulder again. "*Shhh!* Jessica — listen."

We both stood still and listened to the chittering sound down on the floor. The pattering feet, like raindrops drumming on a window. A soft squeak.

Ryan pointed. "There's something moving in

the straw," he said. He dropped to his knees to get a better look.

I dropped down beside him. In the dusty light that filtered through the cracks I saw dark creatures scamper under the straw piles . . . over them . . . across the floor. Creatures darting in all directions.

It didn't take me long to realize they were *rats*!

Dozens of rats, skittering over the straw, dragging their tails over the floor, squeaking and chittering.

"Ohhh, I *hate* rats!" I cried. I jumped to my feet.

Straw clung to the front of my robe. I didn't bother to brush it away. I backed up to the shack wall, trying to move away from the darting, running rats.

"Let's get out of here!" Ryan shouted.

We both lurched toward the door. But before we could get there, it swung open.

I gasped as a ragged-looking man appeared in the doorway. He had a curly brown beard. He wore a long robe that hung down to his bare ankles.

He stepped inside and slammed the door shut behind him.

23

Ryan and I pressed ourselves against the shack wall. I watched in shock as rats began to scamper to the man.

He bent down, and they climbed up his legs. Squealing and squeaking excitedly, they swarmed over him. They covered his arms and legs and clung to the front of his ragged robe.

"So, you're glad to see Simon!" the man cried in a deep voice. He laughed a booming laugh.

The rats perched on his shoulders and held on to his arms. Rats swarmed over his whole body.

He laughed again. "Well, Simon is glad to see you, too!" he cried.

And then his eyes stopped on Ryan and me. He jumped to his feet, sending several rats toppling to the floor.

"Well, well," he said. "And who might you be?"

My brain did flip-flops. What should I tell this man? How could I explain what Ryan and I were doing in his house?

"We . . . uh . . . we are visitors from a faraway land," I stammered.

He brushed rats off his sleeves and took a lumbering step toward us. "And what might you be doing in the Prince's rat house?" he demanded.

Rat house?

"Well . . . we got lost," Ryan spoke up. "We were looking for someone to show us the way."

The man studied us for a long moment. He tugged a rat that had become tangled in his heavy beard and set it down gently on a straw pile.

"You came to the wrong house," he said, frowning at us. "I am Simon, the Prince's Rat Tender."

Rats circled his bare feet. He brushed several more off the front of his robe.

"Why does the Prince have a Rat Tender?" I asked.

"The Prince likes his rats," Simon replied. "Because he feeds them to his cats."

We both stared at him. "Cats?"

Simon nodded. "The Prince has five hundred cats. They get very hungry. That's why he needs me to tend the rats."

He snickered. "The poor things think I am their friend because I feed them every day. They don't realize I am only fattening them up."

He stepped up to Ryan and me. "Here. Have some rats," he said.

He scooped up a bunch of them. Then he dropped them onto my shoulders. They clung to the front of my robe.

"Get them off of me!" I screamed.

I turned and saw Simon drop two or three rats into Ryan's hands. Ryan fumbled with them. He juggled them as if he were doing a circus act.

"Yes, the Prince likes his rats!" Simon boomed. He tossed back his head and laughed.

More rats climbed up the front of my robe. A couple of them slipped inside my hood. I felt their warm bodies rub against my face.

"Help! Please! They're clawing my scalp!" I shrieked. "Help me! Get them out of my hair!"

24

Simon didn't move. The rats all began to screech.

A rat tail brushed over my forehead. I tugged at the rat, but it clung to the inside of my hood.

Ryan spun around to me and pulled the hood down to my shoulders. Then he grabbed the rat and tossed it to the floor.

I wrapped my fingers around another rat and tugged it off my head.

The screeching was deafening. Rats raced back and forth over our feet.

Simon just stood watching the whole thing with a broad smile under his curly beard.

The rats were no longer in my hair, but I could still feel them. My scalp tingled and my skin itched like crazy.

I pushed Ryan toward the door. "Let's go."

We bolted past Simon. Ryan lowered his shoulder and bulled into the door. It burst open, and we tore out of there.

"Do not let the rats escape!" Simon boomed behind us. "The Prince likes his rats!" He slammed the door hard.

Ryan and I didn't look back. We lowered our heads and ran along the backs of the shacks. I could still hear the rats screeching behind us.

We ducked around tall bales of hay. A group of ragged kids was playing some kind of kick-ball game with a small round rock. They stopped as we charged past them.

"Slow down," Ryan said, holding me back. "No one is chasing us. If we keep running, we'll look suspicious."

I stopped and leaned over with my hands on my knees, trying to catch my breath. "Where are we?" I asked.

We both glanced around. I was surprised to see we were back at the blacksmith's stable. Flames danced into the air from his fire. But he wasn't at the fire.

Ryan and I peered around the side of the stable and saw him through the entrance. He was shoeing a horse. The hot tongs glowed red as he pressed the burning horseshoe onto the horse's hoof.

Another horse looked on from the back of the stable. At the side, I saw a tall pile of straw.

The horseshoe sizzled as the powerful man attached it to the horse's hoof.

Ryan and I ducked out of the doorway. I knew we both had the same thought. The stable was the last building on the castle grounds. If we could get past it, maybe we could run to the wall. Maybe we could get back over to the other side. And then we could try the coin again.

Ryan scratched the sleeve of his robe. "Still itchy," he whispered.

I motioned toward the wall. I pulled the hood low on my head and started to walk past the stable.

But a voice boomed: "You there! Halt!"

The blacksmith. He raised the burning tongs as he turned to us.

Ryan made a gulping sound. We both froze in the stable doorway.

Maybe the robes would fool him.

He let go of the horse's hoof and stood up. He kept the long tongs raised at his side. He mopped his forehead with the back of his massive arm. Then he squinted at us.

"I thought I saw the guards take you prisoner," he growled.

He took a step toward us.

"Uh . . . no," I stammered. "It was a mistake. We are guests of Prince Warwick."

He stared at Ryan, then at me. I could see him thinking about that.

Then he motioned with the tongs. "Come into the stable," he said.

I knew we couldn't outrun him. Ryan and I obeyed. I led the way inside. The horse raised its head and let out a soft whinny.

The blacksmith waved us closer. "Back to the wall," he said.

Ryan and I stumbled into the tall pile of straw.

"Keep going," the blacksmith ordered. "Back to the wall. Then sit down in the straw."

"Why?" I asked in a trembling voice. "What are you going to do?"

"I am going to summon the guards," he replied. "I will quickly find out if you are telling the truth."

Ryan and I backed through the straw. Ryan frantically scratched at his hood. Something was definitely bothering him.

"Sit down!" the blacksmith shouted. "Now!"

We both sat down hard. We sank into the straw.

The blacksmith waved the heavy tongs at us. "Do not move," he ordered.

"But — but —" I sputtered. "If you would just let us be on our way . . ."

And then Ryan whispered, "I'm sitting on something."

He reached deep into the straw.

Then he uttered a cry as he pulled up a human head!

25

A man's head. Cut off neatly at the neck. Eyes shut. Scraggly black hair flowing down the back.

The Prince's missing head!

My breath caught in my throat. I started to choke.

Ryan's face turned kind of green. He had a sick expression on his face. He held the head up by the hair.

"Put that down!" the blacksmith boomed.

"We . . . we need this!" I blurted out. I jumped to my feet.

"That stays where it is," he said. "That does not leave the stable."

I grabbed the head from Ryan. My hand brushed the cheek. Cold as ice, the skin as tight as leather.

I felt a wave of nausea. I swallowed hard again and again. I mean, I was *holding a human head*!

Ryan jumped up beside me.

"Heed my words," the blacksmith snarled. "You are not leaving the stable with that."

"The Prince needs this," I said. "The Prince sent us out to find this."

"No, he did not," the blacksmith shot back. "Drop it. Drop it back into the straw. Drop it *now* — if you want to leave this stable alive!"

I gripped the head with both hands. Ryan and I took a few steps toward the open door.

"We're taking this to the Prince," I said. I tried to sound calm. But my voice came out tiny and weak.

We took another step toward the doorway.

The blacksmith let out an angry roar and came at us. He dove forward swinging the big tongs in front of him like a baseball bat.

Ryan and I were trapped. No way to dodge around him.

I let out a scream and ducked as the tongs swung above my head.

I spun around. And saw something crawl out of the sleeve of Ryan's robe.

A rat. No. Two rats.

"I *knew* something was itching me!" Ryan exclaimed.

The blacksmith stopped in his tracks when he saw the two fat gray creatures. They crawled out from Ryan's sleeve and dropped to the straw on the stable floor. Then they turned and went scampering toward the two horses.

Ryan and I stood frozen and watched as the horses went crazy. They both began whinnying frantically, raising up on their hind legs.

The rats darted past them. The horse nearest the door let out a shrill cry — and went galloping from the stable.

"Whoa! Whoooaah!" the blacksmith roared. He heaved the tongs across the stable. Then he spun away from us and chased after the runaway horse.

This was our chance. Ryan and I took off, running full speed out of the stable. We ran past the flaming forge. Turned and headed toward a row of trees that led to the castle.

I gripped the head by its hair. It swung in front of me as we ran.

We hid behind a fat white tree trunk. We were both panting like dogs.

I stuck my head out from behind the trunk and saw a squad of guards marching past the stable.

"Wh-what are we going to do?" Ryan stammered. He gazed down at the head. "We have the Prince's head, Jessica. But how will we ever find the Prince?"

I thought for a moment. Then I said, "Easy. I know how."

I hid the head under my robe. Then I stepped into the open and shouted: "Guards! Hey, guards! Here we are! Come capture us!"

26

"Jessica, you're a genius!" Ryan exclaimed as the guards led us into the castle. The torches along the wall flamed high as if greeting us.

The guards guided us through chamber after chamber. I suddenly had a frightening thought.

"If they take us straight to the dungeon," I whispered, "we'll never get the Prince's head back to him." I swallowed. "Maybe I'm *not* a genius."

We passed through a portrait gallery. Dark paintings of unhappy-looking kings and princes stared out at us. I saw a painting of a sad boy with blond bangs holding a rag doll in his lap.

The next chamber was crowded and noisy. Silver shields hung on the walls, covering them almost completely. Men in red-and-black robes stood in the center of the room, arguing loudly.

The guards didn't stop there. They marched us through the room.

Ryan grabbed my arm. "Jessica, look," he whispered. He pointed to the edge of the crowd.

I gasped when I saw the Duke of Earle and Henway. They were easy to spot. They were the only ones in purple robes.

They were busy arguing with the others — shouting and gesturing. They didn't turn around. They didn't see us.

The guards forced us down a long hallway. Candles flickered brightly from the huge chandelier above our heads.

I moved toward the guard at the front. Beneath his red hat, he had straight blond hair that fell to his shoulders. And a blond mustache to match.

"Where are you taking us?" I asked.

Please . . . I thought. *Please don't say you're taking us to the dungeon!*

"Please!" I begged. "Where are we going?"

The guard's pale blue eyes stared straight ahead. "The Prince wants to see you," he said.

I let out a sigh of relief.

A few minutes later, we entered the Prince's chamber. He sat at his writing desk. His quill moved quickly over a long sheet of parchment. I stared at the stump of a neck poking up from his ruffled shirt collar.

The guards marched us right up to his table.

"Your Excellency," the head guard said, "we have captured the assassins "

The Prince kept writing for a few moments. Then he set down his quill. He turned his headless body toward us.

"Excellency," said the guard, "do you want these prisoners put to death?"

I didn't give the Prince a chance to write a reply. I burst free of the guards and pulled the head from under my robe.

"Prince Warwick, Ryan and I have returned your head!" I shouted.

The Prince's whole body jerked in surprise. He shuddered so hard, he nearly toppled off the tall-backed chair.

I reached the head up to him. "Here. Here it is. I'm putting it in your hands," I said.

He grabbed the head eagerly. He wrapped his fingers around it. Then he smoothed the cheeks with one hand.

He ran his fingers through the tangles of long black hair. Then his hands carefully examined the nose and the dry, pale lips.

"Your Excellency, we don't want a reward," Ryan said. "We only want to go free."

"Yes," I said. "He's right. We didn't do this for any reward. We only want to go home."

The Prince let the head fall to the table. Then he picked up his writing quill and began to scribble furiously. When he finished, he held up what he had written to us:

THIS ISN'T MY HEAD.

27

The head rolled off the table and landed at my feet with a dull *thud*.

I jumped back with a startled cry. Ryan's mouth hung open in shock.

The Prince turned to his parchment, leaned low over the table, and began writing again. After a few moments, he held it up for us to read:

I KNOW THAT HEAD. THE HEAD OF AN ENEMY. MY ENEMIES ALL LOSE THEIR HEADS IF THEY ENTER MY KINGDOM. WERE YOU TRYING TO FOOL ME? NOW IT WILL BE YOUR TURN AT THE CHOPPING BLOCK.

"No!" I cried. "We didn't know! We weren't trying to fool you!"

The blond guard made a grab for me. I spun away and started to run. Ryan lowered his shoulders and ran right behind two guards.

The room filled with angry shouts and cries.

Boots thudded hard on the floor as the guards chased after us.

I pushed open the door and tore out of the room. I peered down the endless red-carpeted hallway. No one there.

"We . . . can't outrun them," Ryan gasped, right behind me.

I knew he was right. We turned a sharp corner. I lifted a heavy purple drape off the wall and ducked behind it. Ryan squeezed in next to me.

I pulled the drape back into place. And held my breath as the guards came pounding down the hall.

I heard them turn the corner. Did they see us?

No. They went thundering past, shouting and cursing.

Ryan didn't move from behind the curtain. We pressed our backs against the wall, breathing heavily.

"Now what?" Ryan whispered. "How do we get out of this castle? How do we get home?"

My mind raced. My brain practically leaped around in my head, jumping with idea after idea.

I realized we had to find the Prince's missing head. That was the only way they would let us go.

I pushed the heavy drape away from my face and turned to Ryan. "I think I know where the head is hidden," I whispered.

"Huh?" His mouth dropped open. "How do you know?"

I peeked out. No one in the hall. I stepped out from behind the drape. It was sweltering back there. I wiped the sweat off my face with both hands.

Ryan followed me out. We kept in the shadows against the wall just in case the guards returned.

"Look around," I whispered. "Do you see any cats?"

Ryan scrunched up his face at me. "Jessica, are you totally losing it?" he demanded. "Why do you want a cat?"

I shook my head. "I don't want a cat. Just look around. Do you see any cats?"

"No," he replied.

"Have you seen any cats in the castle?"

"No."

"We've been chased or dragged or marched through chamber after chamber," I said. "We've been in the Prince's private chamber twice. And we haven't seen a single cat — right?"

Ryan pulled off his sunglasses and rubbed the bridge of his nose. Then he narrowed his dark eyes at me. "Jessica . . . I'm beginning to see what you're saying."

"Yes. You got it. That creepy guy Simon? The guy in the rat shack? He lied to us," I said.

"You're totally right," Ryan said. "He said he

kept his house full of rats to feed the Prince's cats. But the Prince doesn't *have* any cats!"

"That means the rats are there for a different reason," I said. "Maybe the rats are there to guard something. Something that is hidden there."

"Like the Prince's head!" we both said at once.

We crept down the endless hallways, searching for a way out of the castle. I kept picturing the piles of straw in that dark shack. Could the assassins have stashed the head in the straw?

They wouldn't want to carry it far. The shack was the nearest one to the castle.

Was Simon really working for the Prince? Or had the assassins paid him to hide the Prince's head?

We burst out of a side door and went running across the yellow dirt toward the row of shacks. I pulled the hood down over my head and prayed that Simon wasn't inside his shack.

Ryan and I stepped up to the shack and pressed our ears against the door.

I listened hard. I could hear the chittering of the rats inside.

A chill ran down my back. Remembering our last meeting with the rats, my skin began to tingle and itch.

Ryan and I opened the door a few inches and peered inside. A hundred glowing black eyes stared back at us. The sight gave me another chill that shook my whole body.

Were we really going back into this rat den?

Yes.

I pulled the door open just wide enough. Ryan and I squeezed into the dimly lit room.

No sign of Simon. I breathed a short sigh of relief.

I pulled the robe tighter and began to slide against the wall toward the back of the shack. Dozens of rats clustered in the center of the room turned to follow me with their eyes.

Rats darted through the piles of straw. Two rats stood near the door, chirping like birds. Were they calling out a warning?

Ryan and I began walking through the straw piles, kicking straw out of the way with our feet. I didn't want to bend down to search. I knew the rats would climb up my arms. I knew they would bite me.

I brushed two rats off the front of my robe. I kicked my way through a tall straw pile. I slid my shoes slowly along the floor, hoping to bump something.

The head.

The rats chirped louder and began to shriek. Our search was exciting them. A dozen rats surrounded Ryan and me, running in wide circles around our legs.

And then my foot hit something hard at the bottom of a pile of straw.

I reached down. Swiped a rat off my arm. Fumbled in the straw. And picked up a burlap bag.

I brushed a clump of straw off it with my fingers. Pulled it open. And stared at a man's head.

The eyes gazed up at me. Round black eyes. The mouth was frozen in a scream of horror. I pushed back the wavy dark hair to get a better look at the face. The hair looked brittle and dry.

The Prince's head?

"Oh, wow!" Ryan cried out. "Oh, wow. I don't believe it! Jessica — you were right! You found it!"

He had to shout over the screeching of the rats.

My stomach heaved.

For the second time in one day, I was holding someone's head!

It took a few seconds to get myself under control. Then I closed the bag and hid it under my robe. "Let's go," I said.

Stepping over the darting, screeching rats, we edged along the wall toward the door. We were inches away when the door swung open and Simon stepped inside.

He raised his eyes to us and scowled. "Where do you think *you're* going?"

28

He took a step into the shack and started to pull the door closed.

But behind him, a boy let out a shrill cry: "*The rats! They're escaping! They're all escaping!*"

Simon uttered a cry of surprise and whirled around. "Who — ?"

That gave Ryan and me our chance. We pushed past Simon — and dove through the open door.

I wrapped my arms in front of my robe to protect the valuable head. And we ran.

I knew we weren't out of danger. But I had to laugh. Ryan's ventriloquism had saved us. Throwing his voice fooled Simon just long enough.

The sun was nearly down. Long shadows stretched in front of us as we made our way to the castle. A cool wind tried to brush us back. Birds cooed and chirped in the trees, preparing for nightfall.

Guards met us at the front entrance and

quickly took us prisoner. They didn't listen to our pleas to see the Prince.

They marched us to the room outside Prince Warwick's chamber.

I gripped the head carefully under the robe. "How long are you keeping us here?" I asked.

Before the guards could answer, I heard footsteps. The Duke of Earle and the Wizard Henway stepped in.

"You two have led us on a merry chase today," the Duke said. He swept a hand back over his bald head. "You are very clever it seems."

"Yes, we are," I said. I couldn't keep a smile from spreading over my face. "We are very clever."

I pulled the burlap bag from under my robe and raised it in front of them. "We found it. We found the head."

"Now we can return it to the Prince," Ryan said.

"No, you cannot," Henway replied gruffly. He frowned at us. "You are not as clever as you think."

"Excuse me?" I said. "Why can't we return it to the Prince?"

The Duke shook his head. "Once Warwick has his head back, he'll figure out that Henway and I are the ones who chopped it off!"

I uttered a cry of shock. Ryan's mouth dropped open but no sound came out.

"We like being in charge of the kingdom," Henway said. "We don't want the head returned. We thought we hid it away in a safe place. Our friend Simon promised us no one would find it."

"The Prince has no idea we were the attackers," the Duke said. "We wore costumes and our faces were masked. We chopped off his head. We tried to bury it. We tried to burn it. We tossed it down a well. But it returned. It always came back."

"We did not know the Prince's magic was so powerful," Henway said. "I taught him too well. His magic is more powerful than mine. That's one reason he had to be destroyed."

"Finally, we hid the head with Simon and his rats," the Duke said. "We did not know what else to do with it."

Henway sighed. "The Prince lived on without

his head. But there is little he can do without a head. That means the Duke and I are the new rulers."

"But you two would not stop. You two insisted on pursuing your quest for the head," the Duke said with an unpleasant sneer. He reached out both hands toward the bag. "I will take that from you now."

"You will not escape again," Henway added. "We do not know who you are or why you entered our kingdom. But you know too much, and you have seen too much. It is time for you meddlers to take leave of us."

He made a sharp chopping motion with one hand.

It made me gasp. I stared into his eyes. They were cold as ice. I knew that he meant it.

The Duke reached again for the head. I pulled it back.

My mind spun. This was our last chance to save ourselves from the executioner's ax.

"How about another toss of the coin?" The words spilled out of my mouth.

The Duke rubbed his chin. He squinted at me. "I am always ready for an interesting bet," he said.

Henway grabbed his sleeve. "I warned you, Alfred!"

The Duke pulled away from the Wizard's grip. "You cannot keep the Prince's head," he told me.

"But if you win, maybe Henway and I will spare your lives again."

"No promises," Henway said.

"And if we lose?" Ryan asked.

Henway made the chopping motion again.

It made my whole body shudder.

I pictured the chopping block on the tower roof. And again I saw the dark-costumed executioner with his enormous ax.

"Let's toss the coin," I said to the Duke.

A thin smile played over his face. It made his long scar turn pink.

I handed the Prince's head to Ryan. Then I reached under the robe and pulled out the two-headed coin.

At least our lives will be spared, I thought.

To my surprise, the Duke reached for the coin. "It is my turn," he said. "Let me toss it this time."

I had no choice. I had to give it to him. But what if he examined it closely?

He tucked the coin into his palm. He didn't look at it. "You call it," he said.

He tossed the gold coin high in the air.

"I call HEADS!" I shouted.

The coin bounced on the carpet and rolled in front of Henway's purple slippers. He stepped back.

And we all gazed down at the coin.

It was TAILS!

30

"No way!" I cried.

The Duke laughed. "I have fast hands, too!" he exclaimed.

He held up my gold coin. It was still tucked in the palm of his hand. He had switched coins on us.

Still laughing, he flipped my coin back to me. "You won't get to use your trick coin again," he said. "I am afraid your heads will be hidden in Simon's shack along with the Prince's head."

I glanced down at the burlap sack. Ryan held it tightly in front of him in both hands.

"Prepare to die," Henway said. He swept his robe around him. "Follow us to the executioner."

He turned and took one step.

And a voice cried out, "Where do you think you are going?"

Ryan let out a startled shout.

The voice came from inside the burlap bag.

Ryan turned to me. "Did you just throw your voice?"

"No!" I cried.

Ryan pulled open the bag. We stared at the head.

The lips . . . the colorless lips . . . they MOVED. And the eyes blinked.

"I have ears," the Prince's head said in a dry, croaky whisper. "Do you think I cannot hear you?"

"But — but —" Henway and the Duke both began to sputter. Their eyes bulged in horror.

"Even from inside this bag, I heard your confession," the head continued. "I heard you both admit your guilt."

"No, Your Excellency," the Duke said in a panicked whisper. "No, we were teasing the children here. We —"

"We would never harm our Prince!" Henway chimed in.

"Silence!" the head commanded.

Both men shrank back.

"When I am reunited with my body," the head said, "I shall send both of you liars to the chopping block!"

"That's why that will never happen," Henway told the head. He leaped at Ryan and wrapped his hands around the bag.

Ryan tried to pull the bag free. But the Wizard kept his grip. The two of them groaned as they had a fierce tug-of-war battle.

The Duke stepped forward to help Henway.

I pointed my finger wildly behind the two men and screamed: "NO! PLEASE! PUT DOWN THAT BATTLE-AX!"

Henway's hands slipped off the head. The two men spun around.

No one there. Just a desperate trick on my part.

Ryan tossed the head to me. And we both lurched right past the two startled men.

Ryan pulled open the door to the Prince's chamber. He held it for me as I ran in carrying the bag with the Prince's head. Then he followed me as we sprinted to the writing desk.

"Here it is!" I cried breathlessly. "Prince Warwick — here is your head!"

And then I gasped.

He was GONE!

31

"Oh, nooo," I moaned.

Behind us, Henway and the Duke came clattering into the chamber. "Stop right there. Both of you!" Henway shouted.

Ryan and I saw an open door. We darted toward it. Out into the night.

We found ourselves on an outdoor balcony. The air felt fresh and cool. A pale half moon hung low above us.

And the headless Prince stood leaning against the stone railing.

"Here is your head!" I cried breathlessly. I pulled it from the bag and shoved into his hands.

The Prince gripped it by the cheeks. He ran his fingers over the nose, the mouth, the forehead. Then he placed the head on his stump of a neck. He twisted it from side to side. All the while, he murmured strange words, magical words, I guess. He pushed the head down hard, twisting it, twisting it . . . murmuring softly. . . .

A few seconds later, the head was attached.

He blinked his eyes several times. He opened and closed his mouth. Testing the head.

Then he stepped past us, back into the chamber, and shouted for his guards. He gave Henway and the Duke a quick bow. "Thank you so much for confessing to your crime," he said. "You made my job much easier."

He turned to the guards who came bursting into the room. "Take these two traitors to the dungeon!"

"But — but —" Henway and the Duke began to sputter again.

They begged and pleaded as the guards dragged them away. The chamber door closed behind them.

The Prince adjusted his head on his neck. He tilted it one way, then the other. He moved his eyebrows up and down.

When he finally turned to us, he had a smile on his lips. "Jessica," he said, "tell me about the coin. The coin you tossed in your wager with the Duke. What is so special about that coin?"

"It's just a joke coin," I said. "It's a fake." I handed it to him. "See? It has two heads."

He studied the coin carefully, turning it between his fingers. Then he smiled. "That is ME on both sides!" he said.

"Huh?" I stared at him. "The face on the coin — it's *you*?"

He nodded. "Yes. It's true."

I thought hard. "That must be why the coin brought us here," I said. "It brought us here to help you."

Prince Warwick straightened his shirt sleeves. He smiled again. "You rescued me from those two evil men," he said. "I am going to give both of you a very big reward."

He looked at the gold coin again. Then he raised his hand and tossed it back to me.

I reached for it. But it flew over my shoulder.

I turned and saw it bounce onto the carpet.

Ryan and I both dove for it. We both reached out and wrapped our fingers around it. At the same time . . . the same time . . .

And I felt that flipping sensation again. First I was dizzy. Then the floor came up to meet me. The bright red carpet shimmered and glowed in front of me . . . over me . . . all around me.

I opened my mouth to scream. But I flipped over fast. No sound came out. The room tumbled in front of me.

I saw the Prince standing beside his writing table, his face confused. And then I didn't see him. I saw a blur of the purple drapes and the red carpet and the flickering chandelier on the ceiling.

Just a blur. All of it a whirling blur as I felt myself toppling over and over.

"Ooof." I landed hard on my back. My breath shot out of my body.

I gasped for breath. And realized I was staring up into a bright blue sky. I was flat on my back on grass, staring up at the sky. Daytime again.

Slowly, I sat up. I saw the school building up ahead.

"We . . . we're back on the playground!" Ryan cried. "Jessica — check it out. We're back! We're back!"

I climbed to my knees. I shook my head hard, trying to shake away my dizziness. I still felt as if I were flipping head over heels, doing cartwheels in the air.

I glanced around at the soccer field . . . the trees lining the street . . . our good old school building. Then I turned to Ryan. "Hey — we didn't get our reward!" I said.

And a voice behind us said, "I'm going to give you your reward right now!"

I spun around.

It was Boomer. And he was waving a big fist in my face.

32

Ryan and I jumped to our feet. I squinted at Boomer. "What time is it?" I asked.

"Lunchtime," Boomer answered. He waved his hand under my chin. "Pay up. I'm starving. Give me your lunch money."

"Boomer, please," Ryan groaned. "We just got back and —"

Boomer grabbed the front of Ryan's T-shirt. He pulled it toward him. I could hear the shirt ripping. "Do you have lunch money for me or not?" he boomed.

I tapped Boomer on the shoulder. "Let's flip for it one more time," I said. "Come on. Flip you for it."

Boomer let go of Ryan. He gave Ryan a hard shove back. Then he turned to me. "Okay. We'll flip for it, Jessica. If you lose, you both give me your lunch money for a month!"

"No problem," I said.

He never learns! I thought.

I pulled out the gold coin. "Here goes," I said. "Heads, I win."

I flipped the coin high in the air. It caught the sunlight as it flew up. Then sank to the grass and landed at Boomer's feet.

We gazed down at it.

TAILS.

I picked up the coin and studied it. Tails on both sides.

The Prince had switched coins! He tricked us!

I guess he wanted the one with his face on it.

Boomer stuck his meaty hand under my face. "You lose — big-time, Jessica. Pay up. Pay up now, or . . . face the Mighty Fisto!"

"You *named* your fist?" I cried. "Oh, never mind. Of course, you did."

Ryan and I reached into our backpacks for our wallets. "Put the Mighty Fisto down, Boomer," I said. "We're paying . . . We're paying!"

EPILOGUE

Ryan and I were broke. And it was going to be hard to skip lunch for a month. But we were so totally happy to be home, it was a small price to pay.

I carried the gold coin around for a couple of days. But none of my friends wanted to make any bets.

After dinner, I went up to my room. I decided to tuck the coin on a shelf where I keep a lot of other magic tricks. But as I crossed my room, I saw a yellow-green glow.

I stopped. My heart skipped a beat. Was something in my bookshelf on fire?

No.

I hurried closer — and saw that it was the little Horror. The tiny figure that Jonathan Chiller had attached to my gift package in his HorrorLand souvenir shop.

Suddenly, Chiller's words repeated in my mind: "*Take a little Horror home with you . . .*"

A ring of bright light radiated off the Horror's body. It glowed brighter as I stared. And the ring of yellow-green light spread out from the figure . . . wrapped around me . . .

. . . Until I felt the warmth of it. A fiery warmth. A bright curtain of light circled me. And then began to pull . . . pull me inside.

I struggled to breathe. But the heat was so intense. The light was so bright, I clamped my eyes shut.

A second later, I opened my eyes. The glow had vanished. I stood in a store aisle. I blinked at cluttered shelves and display cases.

"How did I get here?" I said out loud. And then I saw I wasn't alone. Standing behind the counter with a strange, unpleasant smile on his wrinkled face — Jonathan Chiller!

"Jessica, welcome back," he said in his croaky voice. His gold tooth gleamed as his smile grew wider.

"But . . . how did I get here? What am I doing here?" I cried.

His smile faded. He narrowed his eyes at me behind his square spectacles. "It's time to pay me for your souvenir," he said softly. "It's time for you to pay, Jessica."

MONDO the MAGICAL

PROFESSION: Magician
REAL NAME: Hairy Houdini
FAVORITE SAYING: "Oops!"
BEST TRICK: Making wallets disappear
PROUDEST ACHIEVEMENT: Pulled a rabbit out of a rabbit

HORRORLAND SPLAT STATS

TRICKS UP SLEEVE:
WOMEN SAWED IN HALF:
WOMEN SAWED IN HALF WHO SURVIVED:
BOOED BY CROWD:
DEAD PIGEONS FOUND IN TOP HAT:

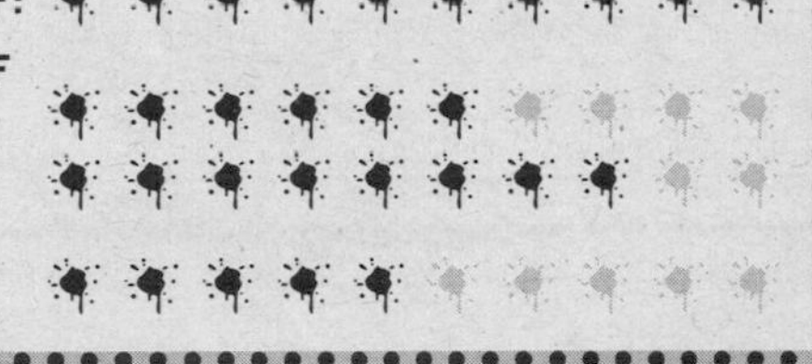

Mondo has been perfecting his magic act at HorrorLand for years. His most famous trick involves pulling a human ear out of a quarter. Unfortunately, he spent two years in prison for that trick. Perhaps his biggest skill as a magician is making audiences disappear as soon as he starts his act.

Ready for more thrills and chills?

Why did Jonathan Chiller bring Jessica back to HorrorLand? What real terrors does he have in store for her?

You'll have to wait for the answers. You won't know Chiller's secret plans until you read all seven books in this new series.

More kids will soon "take a little Horror home with them." Meg Oliver will be next. You'll meet Meg in Goosebumps HorrorLand #16: a double-sized super-special edition called *Weirdo Halloween.*

When you read that book, you'll take a little horror home with YOU! And — you'll be one step closer to the most terrifying HorrorLand adventure of them all!

31

I expected to see my empty bookshelves. My totally wrecked and messed-up room.

But no. I was standing in a brightly lit store. Hunched in a narrow aisle between high cluttered shelves. I saw grinning skulls . . . a two-headed monkey . . . a fortune-teller's crystal ball . . . giant rubber cockroaches.

"Oh, wow," I muttered. I knew where I was.

I didn't *believe* it. But I knew where I was. Back in Chiller House. Back in HorrorLand.

I heard a cough. I turned to see Jonathan Chiller step out from behind the counter.

His balding head gleamed under the store lights. He peered at me through the square glasses perched on the end of his nose. When a smile slowly crossed his face, his gold tooth glimmered.

"Welcome back, Meg," he croaked in his old-man voice. He took a step toward me.

I took a step back — and bumped into a giant stuffed Godzilla.

"What's going on?" I cried in a trembling voice. "How did I get here?"

His smile grew wider. The shoulders of his old-fashioned brown suit rose up and down. "Magic," he said softly.

He reached for the little Horror. I didn't even realize I still had it gripped tightly in my hand. I handed it to him. He tucked it into his pants pocket.

"I . . . I don't understand," I stammered. "Why did you do this? Why did you bring me back here? Didn't that ugly Floig cause me enough trouble?"

He motioned with one hand. "Take a deep breath, Meg. You are perfectly safe here. I know you've had a surprising time."

"*Surprising?*" I screamed. "You call it *surprising*? It . . . it was *horrible*! I want to go home — now!"

Again he motioned for me to calm down. "*Shhhh.* You're going to have fun," he said in a whisper. "I brought you here for fun."

I swallowed hard. My mouth was dry as sand. "Fun?"

He swept a hand back over his thinning hair. "Halloween is the most exciting time of all at HorrorLand," he said. "The park is a huge Halloween party. I thought you would enjoy it."

"You grabbed me from my house and pulled me here through some kind of weird magic so I could enjoy Halloween at HorrorLand?" I rolled my eyes. "Tell me another one. What is this *really* about?"

"I'm telling the truth," Chiller said softly. "I love to play games, Meg. I had a lonely childhood. I spent day after day in my room, making up all kinds of games."

I stared hard at him. "Boo hoo," I said. "Will you please send me home now?"

He ignored my question. "I thought you might like to come back here and play a game, too," he said.

I crossed my arms tightly in front of me. "What kind of game?"

His gold tooth gleamed. "A masquerade game," he said. "You know. For Halloween."

"I don't *think* so," I said. "Thanks, anyway. I've already celebrated Halloween. How about you send me home now?"

Chiller picked up a stuffed python and pulled it back and forth through his hands. "Don't worry, Meg. I'll send you home safe and sound," he said. "I promise. I'm not a bad man. I just like to share my games with others."

I stared hard at him. "Not interested."

The stuffed python slid through his hands. "It's an easy game," Chiller said. "You just have to do one thing to win."

I rolled my eyes. "One thing? What? What do I have to do?"

His expression grew serious. "Prove that you are you," he said.

32

"Excuse me?"

My mouth dropped open. I leaned back against the counter. "You want to see my I.D.?" I said. "My school I.D.? I don't have it with me. I didn't know I was coming here, remember? I didn't think I'd have to bring I.D.!"

The words tumbled out of me. My heart was thudding so hard in my chest, I could barely hear myself think.

Chiller set the stuffed python down next to a pile of plastic spiders. "No. No need for an I.D. card," he said. "That won't help you, Meg. This is a game."

I took a deep breath and let it out slowly. Outside the shop, I heard kids laughing and shouting to each other.

"The game is called *Double or Nothing*," Chiller said.

I crossed my arms tighter over my chest. "I told you — I don't want to play."

About the Author

R.L. Stine's books are read all over the world. So far, his books have sold more than 300 million copies, making him one of the most popular children's authors in history. Besides Goosebumps, R.L. Stine has written the teen series Fear Street and the funny series Rotten School, as well as the Mostly Ghostly series, The Nightmare Room series, and the two-book thriller *Dangerous Girls*. R.L. Stine lives in New York with his wife, Jane, and Minnie, his King Charles spaniel. You can learn more about him at www.RLStine.com.

R. L. Stine's Fright Fest—

Now with Splat Stats and More!

Read them all!

SCHOLASTIC

www.scholastic.com/goosebumps

GBCLS16